THE 1776 MUSKET

BY

LOUISE HARRIS

DEDICATION

This book is dedicated to my readers who have pushed me to have a sequel and to those hard-working librarians who seem to be forgotten as more books and periodicals are becoming electronic and duties are automated.

CHAPTER 1
THE DATE

The woman was proud of her work. She stood back from the table to admire what she had done. The bomb wasn't visible when looking at the 1776 musket. She dated the man whose father had collected historical weapons. She stole it to create her bomb. Her plan was taking shape. *People must pay. All of them must be punished. I just need more time.*

She circled Feb. 14 on her calendar because that date was special to her. That was the date she and her brother were separated a few years ago. She had searched for him for years. When she finally found him, he was not his former self. He barely talked. He is angry all the time. He doesn't recognize her. He doesn't smell like he did when they were kids. Now, the world must pay for taking her from her brother. *Yes. Feb. 14 is the day I start punishing people.*

The woman shivered. She wore a thin jacket and a plain blue short-sleeve shirt over her torn jeans. They were not nearly sufficient for February in Philadelphia, but they will have to do. She could not afford anything else. She worked in the campus book store. She got the job after another employee found a better position. She liked it for her purposes. She could watch people at the book store and blend into the crowd. No one cared much about store personnel. She liked it that way.

Stocking shelves allowed her to hear all kinds of things that people would normally keep to themselves. For example, on Feb. 14, the University of Pennsylvania is honoring the first of those who need punishing for her dedicated service to the school's library system. Many dignitaries will be there. It will be the perfect place for the woman's plan. Many of the people who go to that party will have to die so she can tell them they are wrong for their treatment of her.

Satisfied with her plan as it was taking shape, the woman

smiled an evil-not-reaching-her-eyes smile. She could have been attractive if it weren't for the scars on her face and hands. She had gotten too close to the whip one of her foster parents used. She looked like she was from Latin America, but she really came from Russia. She was a Gypsy. Her mother brought her and her brother to the states. When it was too difficult to care for them, she dumped them in a trash can. They were alone and on the streets until the government stepped into their business and put them in foster care. Then, the whippings came.

However, she did have relationships, including the one that the bastard recently ended. *They must all die.*

CHAPTER 2
THE STUDENT

Floralynda waited on the library steps for Annie who was expected from her class. Her long chestnut hair was blowing in the breeze. She shivered despite her parka, hat and gloves. She never got warm in the winter. She blamed her mother who grew up in Miami. She knew her blood was wired for warmer climates. She will have to move after she graduates from Penn, but that was three years away. Until then, she must endure Philadelphia winters, which weren't as bad as any place farther north.

"Lynn," Annie yelled and waved.

"I hate winter," Floralynda said as her friend got closer.

"Why didn't you wait inside the library?"

"I didn't want to miss you and besides, the library must have the heat up to 100 degrees. It's stifling in there."

"Guess what?" Annie queried.

"What?"

"We have a new TA in the history department. He's so hot."

"Why are you drooling over a teacher? It's not a good idea to get involved with a professor."

The strawberry-blonde smiled a devilish smile into Lynn's sapphire blue eyes.

"I wouldn't dream of dating a teacher or betray Sam, but you are a computer geek. You'll never have him as a teacher."

"Stop trying to fix me up. I don't want to date any other

man after Chris," she countered piercing Annie's golden eyes with blue fire. In a softer tone, she added, "I do have to take some noncomputer classes, and it's still not a good idea for me to go after a teacher."

"Technically, he's only a few years older than you."

"Come on, Annie. Let's get out the cold and work on your history research project."

Lynn and Annie stood in line to ask the librarian a question. She was in her 40s with curly blonde hair that had streaks of brown and looked like a chocolate chip cookie on her head. She had been at the university library for 25 years. Signs all over the library talked about a reception in her honor and fund-raising event on Valentine's Day. Every time, Lynn talked with her she wanted to laugh because she heard rumors about her that she was an incredible flirt.

"Hello girls. What can I do for you today?" Cookie Stockton asked.

"We need information on the history of technology," Annie said. "I have to write a timeline piece on the evolution of phones and computers to today."

"Wow. That's a broad topic."

"I tried to tell her," Lynn said.

"Well, I was going to just do computers, but Lynn pointed out that we needed phones before we could have computers. She also reminded me that phones' and computers' functions are blurring today and must be lumped together."

"Don't worry. I'll get you books for you to start. I'm sure you can narrow it during your writeup. Come back tomorrow," Cookie suggested.

"Thanks, Cookie. You're always so helpful," Lynn said.

"Tell my niece, please. She thinks I don't help at all," she laughed.

Annie and Lynn left for the food court in the book store building. Annie grabbed Lynn's arm as they walked into the cold air again.

"What?"

"There he is! He's heading right for the library!"

"You know the library is open to professors too," Lynn sneered, but she got a good look at the new teaching assistant. He had charcoal black hair, brown eyes so dark they looked almost black, but they held compassion and lightness. Lynn felt no fear when she looked in his eyes. He walked with confidence and wore jeans, a green turtleneck shirt and a heavy sweatshirt. His chest could be as wide as the Ben Franklin Bridge, although it was hard to tell due to the bulky clothes. Lynn immediately felt an attraction to him.

"You're right. He's good-looking, but he's still a TA."

They walked away. As they left, Lynn considered the man and knew without a doubt she would be warm in his arms.

CHAPTER 3
THE TEACHING ASSISTANT

Solomon Adams walked up the library steps. He smiled to his student, a smile that transformed his face into one that showed how much he enjoyed life. He liked her. She was studious, answered his questions and genuinely wanted to learn. So many other students were at the University of Pennsylvania because their rich parents expected it. He wondered who her knockout friend was. Her hair caught the sun and reminded him of a poinsettia flower. He noticed she was cold and thought how nice it would be to warm her, but he reminded himself that she was a student.

Still, he imagined rubbing his hands down her slim waist and slender legs. He shook his head to break the spell she cast over him. He thought about how she smiled at her friend. It was soft and full of life and spirit. *I have to stop these thoughts.*

"Hello, Ms. Stockton. I am ..."

"You're new here, aren't ya," Cookie said.

"Um, yes. I graduated in December from Rutgers. I'm here for graduate school," Sol said uncomfortably due to the way Cookie eyed him like he was a meal for a starving wolf.

"Well, Sugar, please call me Cookie. I get off at five," she said with a clear double entendre. "My house is on Chestnut Street. Come by so I can welcome you to Philly properly."

"Um. Thanks, but I grew up in Upper Darby and am quite familiar with Philly. I think I'll find what I need myself."

"Are ya sure?" Again with double meaning.

Sol didn't know if she was talking about the invitation or

his library needs and decided not to ask. He just left the desk and headed for another part of the library. He found a bulletin board with the information he sought – names of history clubs on campus, re-enactment clubs and collectors. Sol's specialty was the Revolutionary War and loved to get involved with groups that supported his love of that era. He enjoyed looking at his father's musket that was past down through his family. He wasn't a collector, though. His father collected weapons from all eras and had bought four muskets. The last time he visited, he noticed one was missing, but he figured his father sold it.

"Hey there," an old man said to Sol.

"Hello, Professor Dickenson. How are you?"

"The cold really affects my old bones. I'll be glad when I retire in June. Gonna move to Arizona. No snow or cold."

"What about the summer? It's 115 degrees in the shade there," Sol said to the man wearing layers of clothing and a scarf.

"I won't mind."

"Professor, about the research paper ..."

"We'll talk about it later. I can't think when I'm not in my office."

Sol nodded. He knew the history professor who he assisted wasn't organized. His office was pure clutter. Yet, he always kept the interest of his students and let them use their imaginations. For example, the research paper. He told them to research the history of anything and write a timeline and 20-page paper on the timeline. Sol anticipated many hours reading, checking for plagarism and verifying dates on 300 different topics. He wished Professor Dickenson had given everyone the same topic. It would have made his life easier, but then, the papers would get monotonous.

"All right. I 'll catch you back at the office. I have a meeting until 3 p.m."

"Good. Good. I have some reading to do here at the library. Maybe flirt with Ms. Stockton."

"Ms. Stockton? You're old enough to be her father."

"She doesn't care. Why should I? Anyway, it's harmless fun, especially when I'm missing my wife. She died, you know, a year ago."

"So you've said many times. Bye Professor."

Sol smiled at the old man and left the library. He headed for the re-enactors meeting.

CHAPTER 4
THE RE-ENACTORS MEETING

The re-enactors meeting was held at the 1776 Inn near Penn's Landing in the dining room. Sol took the El downtown and took a seat in the first chair he saw. About 40 people had braved the cold to attend. The president called the meeting to order.

"All right. Come to order. We have a few new faces I see. Welcome. Our secretary is sick with the flu so no minutes will be taken unless someone volunteers."

No one did. The door to the dining room flew open. Sol recognized the woman who entered. He decided the boring meeting just got more lively.

"I'm sorry I'm late. My father asked me to take notes on the meeting for your minutes," she said.

"My God. You can't be little Lynn Binary? I haven't seen you in years!" the president exclaimed.

"As you can see John, I am all grown up now. Studying computer programming at Penn."

"How's your father?"

"He's really sick. He can't keep anything down."

Sol decided to end this conversation before he lost his lunch.

"Sir, I thought you were about to start?"

"That's right. So Lynn, you'll take the minutes?"

"Yes."

Sol nearly jumped when she scanned the room and looked at him. She walked, carrying her laptop and sat in the chair next to him.

"Hi. I might need you to keep me awake. I came with my dad once and quickly lost interest. I was so bored that I fell asleep when I couldn't understand them."

Sol laughed. "I'm Solomon, but all my friends call me Sol. I'll help all I can. I wouldn't want you to embarrass your dad by falling asleep and missing the important stuff for the minutes."

Her laughter was pleasurable. It lit up her whole face like flower petals in the sun. *Stop this. She's a student*, Sol told himself. "I'm Lynn Binary."

"So what brings you here?"

Sol wasn't sure he wanted to tell her he actually enjoyed these things, but he decided to be honest anyway.

"I specialize in the Revolutionary War history. I love re-enacting battles and being around others who do also."

Lynn smiled. "Everyone is allowed to be happy. I'm glad you like it. You'll fit right in with my dad." She cringed. That would mean a long-term relationship for him to get to know her dad, but, of course, he was a member. "How do you like teaching at Penn?"

"Most of the students want to learn. Professor Dickenson is an coot who gives me a lot of freedom. I like that. I think he's grooming me for when he retires in June."

Lynn typed on her laptop computer notes of the president's and treasurer's reports. She added notes of the questions and recorded the votes. The president then discussed locations, dates and times of the re-enactments. Lynn took notes of those. Sol watched her throughout the meeting. He studied her slender fingers as they flew across the keyboard. He imagined those fingers on his chest and became uncomfortable.

"Are you going to participate?"

"Huh?" Sol asked. *Participate? I would love to participate. Wait! She meant the re-enactment.*

"Probably. The first event is near the end of the semester. I might be busy with papers."

"You're probably right if my friend's paper is an indication of what you have to look forward to in the papers. Her topic is broad."

"I saw you with Annie at the library. Are you taking any history classes?"

"Thank God, no." She blushed. "I mean, it's OK if you and Annie like it."

"I'm not offended. Not everyone can like history. For me, it comes alive when I walk in the footsteps of people who lived it."

"I prefer to meet people online instead of face-to-face. Give me artificial intelligence any day."

Her face shone like gold as she discussed her passion for computers. He could see it in her eyes. He admired her more, but cautioned himself.

"You have no problem talking to me."

"I can be social, but I live for the cyber world."

"I see that. You're whole face brightens." *Stupid Jerk. Why did you say that?*

"Thank you. You are nice," Lynn supplied by rote.

Now, she thinks I like her, which I do, but I can't have her.

Lynn resumed her note-taking. When the meeting ended, she said, "It was nice talking to you. I enjoyed this meeting more than I expected."

Me too. "Bye, Lynn. Good luck in the semester."

As Lynn walked out the door, Sol watched her movements just a little too long. He shook his head, gathered his folder, papers and briefcase and took the El to Penn for class.

CHAPTER 5
THE FANTASIES

Lynn thought of nothing else but the muscular, handsome teaching assistant at the meeting during her drive back to campus. He had a compassionate smile and genuinely seemed interested in what she had to say. She allowed herself the fantasies because she knew nothing would come between them. He was a teacher. She was a student. She vowed to stay away from men after Chris nearly violated her. She shivered.

"I hope you rot in Hell."

"What?" her roommate asked.

"Sorry, Annie. I was thinking about Chris. I want him to rot. Not you. I didn't know I said that out loud."

"Where have you been?"

"Dad asked me to take notes at his re-enactors meeting. He's so sick."

"I thought you hate those things."

"True, but Dad needed me to go. Anyway, I'm glad I did."

Annie was puzzled.

"Guess who was there?" Lynn interjected.'

"Who?"

"The T.A. you were so jazzed about."

"Really? What happened?"

"Annie, stop thinking like that. We just talked! That's all."

Annie frowned.

"Are you going to see each other again?"

"It wasn't a date, and he's a teacher. We did have fun at the meeting. He's nice. He goes by Sol."

"Lynn, don't give up. You might find a way to get together."

"Annie, you're a hopeless romantic. Don't you have to work on your project?"

"I suppose, but I'd rather talk some more."

"I'm done talking about Sol. I have to write a computer program for class tomorrow."

The two worked in silence on papers and projects. Visions of Sol in a Revolutionary uniform kept popping into Lynn's mind. Every now and then, Lynn would imagine herself as the maiden giving water to the soldiers. She smiled as she worked on her studies. She was never going to tell Annie how much she fantasized about Sol. That was her secret. Occasionally, she caught Annie grinning and suspected she knew what was in Lynn's head.

"Why don't you ask him to the library reception? You could go as a teacher and student who both happen to want to support Ms. Stockton. And, you could claim you wanted protection because you don't want to walk alone in the city," Annie suggested.

"Will you quit it? I don't need a matchmaker."

"You could meet him there. That would be innocent."

"Stop. Just stop. I won't date a teacher."

"It's just so Romeo and Juliet."

"They both died, you know," Lynn said hoping that would convince Annie to drop the subject.

Secretly, she liked the idea – a chance encounter at a reception where a lot of boring people would be there. She thought about her conversation at the 1776 Inn and imagined laughing at the boring people while talking in their own world. She sighed. She couldn't have Sol. She didn't want Sol or any man. She went back to computer programming.

CHAPTER 6
THE MUSKET

The woman smiled. The musket bomb was finished. She had only to deliver it to the library to start her revenge. She scowled. The last conversation with her brother came back.

"Christoph, what happened?'

"She fired me. Caught me doing stuff to the books."

"What will you do?"

"I applied for a job with a warehouse on the river."

"We need to pay rent."

"Stop it. I know our situation. You don't have to keep harping on it."

She slapped his face.

"Don't you dare talk to me that way."

He grabbed a book and threw it at her. It hit her head and she heard, "I'm done with you. I'm outta here."

She swayed and hit the edge of a table. She blacked out from the injuries. When she came back, he was gone. She searched for him at the usual spots. The bartender said he came in and drank. He left after that.

"He left you a napkin."

Katrina, I'm sorry. I have to go. I'll be back with money.

But, he never came back. If that Bitch didn't fire him, they would still be together. She visited the library for six months to find the perfect place for the musket. She decided the center room would inflict the most damage. During those six months, she researched how to build a bomb and how to make it fit in a musket. It had to be a musket because the library often had Revolutionary War exhibits in February. Now, her hard work has been completed. *They will pay!*

She walked to the library in the disguise of an old woman.

"Hello. Welcome to University of Pennsylvania's Library. How can I help you?" the clerk said.

"Good morning. I'm moving into a nursing home, and I need to clean out my house. I'd like to donate this musket from 1776 to the library in honor of George's Washington's birthday," Katrina said in an older raspy voice.

"Wow. That's nice. The gun is in great shape. Let me show you where to put it," the clerk said.

Katrina followed and placed the gun on a pedestal of glass in the middle room. She quickly left.

"Let me get your information for the plaque," the clerk said, but Katrina was gone.

CHAPTER 7
THE POSSIBILITIES

Sol tried to concentrate on the lesson. Professor Dickenson droned on about the necessary reasons for a flag and an identity. Sol constantly got distracted. He couldn't stop thinking about the sexy computer programming student. Lynn's laughter continued to ring in his head. His mind thought about those lips and her smile. *How I want to taste those lips*. He shook his head.

"Sol, you don't agree?"

He realized that Professor Dickenson asked him a question.

"I'm sorry, Professor. There was a fly near me. I shook my head to get it away from me. What was the question?"

"I asked whether you agree that Colonial America couldn't decide which flag to use and that put the colonies at a disadvantage."

"Right. Disadvantage because there was no unity. That comes much later."

The class continued, but Sol barely listened. He kept a careful ear out for any direct questions aimed his way, but his mind was elsewhere. He would look at Annie and think about Lynn. Or he would imagine Lynn dressed as Betsy Ross. Sometimes, he thought about her as a tavern wench. *Stop this*, he told himself for the 100th time. *She's a student*.

After class, Annie came up to him.

"Mr. Adams, I have a question about the research project."

"What is it?"

"Can we use drawings and photographs from the Internet? I can't draw very well."

"Of course, just make sure they are free of copyrights and cite the source."

"Good. Are you going to the reception tomorrow night?"

"Annie, are you asking me out?"

"No. I'll be going with my boyfriend, Sam. I was just curious about whether you were going."

"I have to go. All TAs are required to attend. Some professors too. It's a big deal. But, I'm not sure I want to be near Ms. Stockton."

"Don't worry about her. She flirts with everybody. Her bed is never empty, I'm told."

"Yeah. I got that impression, but I don't want to sleep with her."

"So don't. She'll find someone else to be her date," Annie said. "I better go. See you there."

Sol grabbed his papers and headed to his office. He sat in his chair staring out the window. *If Annie is going, I wonder if Lynn is going. I could talk with her without a problem and on Valentine's Day too! I like this plan. A date without anyone knowing it's a date.*

"You did what?" Lynn asked.

"I asked if he was going to the reception."

"Annie, are you insane? I can't date him. He's a teacher. When are you going to stop this matchmaking."

"Never. Besides, I know you like him. And, the beauty of this is that you're not dating him. You are meeting him at a reception with lots of teachers milling about the students. No one will question why you're there!"

"Annie, I don't care. I'm not going to the reception just to meet him. I might not go at all. It probably will be boring."

"You told Cookie you would."

"Yes. Well, I think I'm getting Dad's illness."

"Coward. Just go. Talk with him. Have fun."

"I could avoid him that night."

"Pity."

"Annie, you're impossible. I don't want or need a man."

"Keep telling yourself that. You might begin to believe it. Still, if you choose to change your mind, that Hotty Professor is a good one for you to change your mind."

"Ugh!"

Lynn left the room. The reception offered possibilities, but she shook her head. He's not for her.

CHAPTER 8
THE MYSTERIOUS HUM

Annie and Lynn walked to the library.

"Hello Cookie," Lynn said.

"Did you find the materials for my project?" Annie said.

Cookie wore a miniskirt and a long-sleeve shirt showing cleavage.

"I have it right here."

She handed Annie a stack of books, periodicals and Web site addresses.

"This should give you enough for your report. You'll have plenty to narrow down the topic."

"Are there maps and pictures in this stack?"

"Of course. And, other graphics."

"Thanks, Cookie. You really saved me time," Annie said.

Lynn had been wandering the library. She noticed the musket.

"What an interesting gun," she said.

"It's a 1776 musket. A local collector donated it to the library because she was cleaning out her house to go into a nursing home. Isn't that something?"

"It's beautiful. My dad's is muddy from using in re-enactments. Who donated it? Maybe Dad knows her."

"I wasn't here at the time, and the clerk didn't get a name."

"Why is it humming?" Annie asked.

"Annie, muskets don't hum. You must be hearing the security in the rare exhibit room," Lynn said. "Or maybe, the heater is humming."

"I guess you're right, Lynn."

Cookie frowned. Something wasn't right, but some students asked her a question so she forgot about the conversation on the musket.

"Bye, Cookie. Thanks. See you at the reception."

As Lynn and Annie exited, Sol entered.

"Hi Sol," Lynn said.
Sol looked at them and smiled. He gave a more meaningful smile to Lynn.

"Hi. Good to see you both."

Lynn knew Sol was checking out her looks and jiggled her butt a little in response. She smiled back with a smile that made her face glow. Then, she stopped herself.

"Do you know where Ms. Stockton is?" Sol asked.

"Last we saw, she was in the rare exhibit section helping several grad students. Why?" Lynn sniped. Annie slapped her.

"Good. I can go into the library, get the books I need and leave without seeing her."

Lynn let out a breath. Annie slapped her again.

"Don't you like her?" Annie asked.

"She's too much for me. I don't like overzealous women."

Lynn and Annie laughed. Sol was charmed by their laughter and joined in the fun. His smile reminded her of the sun on a warm day. She liked that feeling, especially because it was winter. Sol always make her feel warmer even when it's in the 20s outside the library.

"Sooner or later, she'll take you to bed. There's not a man on campus she hasn't had," Annie said. Lynn slapped Annie.

Lynn gazed into his eyes and realized Sol was frightened and worried about that prospect.

"Well, Annie is exaggerating a little, but she is a flirt."

"I found that out already. Hence, the reason I want to avoid her," Sol replied.

"Well, we better get going, then. Otherwise, she'll be back at her desk."

"Right."

Lynn and Annie started to leave when Sol called them back.

"Wait. Lynn are you … Never mind. See ya later."

Sol went into the library.

"What do you think he was going to ask?"

Annie smiled a devious grin. "I don't know, Lynn, but you got jealous there for a second."

"No I didn't."

"Yes you did."

"Oh, all right, maybe, I did. It doesn't matter if I'm jealous. I am not seeing him and won't be seeing him. I have to get to class. Catch you for dinner."

Lynn headed for class while Annie went to her dorm room to read through the material.

CHAPTER 9
COOKIE'S ATTACK

Sol went to the history section. He wanted references for a paper he was doing for one of his grad school classes. He also needed some new material to present in his undergraduate classes. He was deeply engrossed in his search and didn't see Cookie Stockton coming up to him until her long slender fingers were feeling his chest. He froze, then turned, looking like a deer caught in headlights.

"Ms. Stockton ..."

"Sugar, call me Cookie."

"Cookie, what are you doing?"

"I thought you were in grad school. Isn't it obvious?"

"I guess I mean, why me?"

"Sugar, don't you know how good-looking you are? You give off an aura of confidence, compassion and protectiveness. Any woman would want you."

"From what I hear, you're not too picky," Sol said scurrying away from her.

"No. I'm not, but I mean it. You're one of the prettier ones. Besides, I want to thank you for the gift."

"Gift? What gift?"

Cookie stroked his arm. Sol felt aroused and frightened at the same time. He also was curious about this gift she mentioned.

"The musket. It arrived yesterday when I was out. Professor Dickenson said you have a 1776 musket, so I figured you must have donated it even though my co-worker said it was an old woman."

"I don't have one. My father is the collector. Where is the one the library received?"

"Right, this way."

Cookie took his arm and led him to the rare objects exhibit. Along the way, she moved her fingers along his arm to his neck. His skin tingled. He couldn't concentrate on what she was telling him.

"Here it is." Her hand massaged his bottom. He gulped.

Sol was so thrown off by Cookie's actions that he didn't figure out the musket was his father's that had been passed down through his family for generations and appeared missing the last time he visited his dad's house. Sol wanted to leave. He could tell this was a maneuver on Cookie's part to get him alone. Even though he was not attracted to Cookie like he was Lynn, her actions would wear down any healthy male. So, he wasn't surprised when she grabbed him and planted a kiss on him. At first, he tried to resist, but he was already in pain. Cookie pressed her body closer to his. Her cleavage rubbed his chest. Her silky thighs and miniskirt enticed his groin, making him give into the kiss. Her hand explored his body, forcing Sol to want more.

"Take me to your office," Sol squeaked.

"All right."

Cookie led him to her office, locked her door and closed the blinds. Cookie yanked off his clothes. She herself was undressed in less than a minute. They had sex on the floor of her office. After a while, Cookie said he had to leave. He was disappointed but understood that this was just a one-time coupling, nothing more.

"Will you want to do it again?" he clarified just in case he was wrong.

"Sugar, I wanted to know what you feel like, and now, I do, but you must know that I don't repeat too often with the same man," Cookie said.

"I had heard that about you," Sol said, nodding.

"Besides, I felt you weren't giving me everything. It felt like you were reserving yourself for someone."

"My future wife, I guess. Whoever that might be."

"I might want you again, but not now."

"Cookie, it's OK. I won't ask again. Anyway, you started this."

"*Touché, mon cherie.*" She smiled, dressed and went to help students.

Sol laid on her office floor for a few minutes more, thinking about what he had done. He wondered about the musket. *Who could have donated it? Why did it look familiar?* What surprised him most was why he feared Lynn's reaction to his pleasuring Cookie. *Why did she pop into my head while was with Cookie?* He got dressed and headed across campus.

CHAPTER 10
PICKING THE CLOTHES

Lynn and Annie looked through their closets. They wanted the right outfits for the reception.

"I don't like any of these, and I don't have time to go home to see what I have there," Lynn said.

"This emerald green dress looks good on you."

"Yes, but I wear that a lot. People have seen me in it many times."

"True. Mr. Adams hasn't, though."

"Annie, I'm not interested in him."

"You're interested, but you don't want to pursue it. There's a difference."

"Let's go shopping and buy a new dress for the reception."

"All right. I don't want to wear any of mine either. I don't have much money."

The young women drove to Liberty Place at Market Street. They entered the upscale shopping center in Center City. They found a department store and headed for the fancy dress section. Lynn found a periwinkle strapless dress with blue and silver sparkles scattered throughout the dress on the clearance rack. She also grabbed a black one with white pearls around the neck. The black one was long-sleeved but the sleeves were lace. The dress buttoned up at the neck.

Annie saw a bright pink dress with red roses in hearts on the shoulders. The one-sleeve dress was slender in the waist but fanned out at the bottom. She also liked a red one with gold on the top. They took their finds to the fitting room to try on the dresses.

"That's nice. It'll keep you warm," Annie commented about Lynn's black choice.

"It's beautiful, but I feel like a nun in this. This library thing is for someone who is definitely not a nun. Therefore, the guests shouldn't be either."

"What do you think of mine?" Annie asked.

"Are you trying to attract Sam or attend a Christmas dinner?" Lynn replied about the red one.

"It's a little plain. I'll go put on the other one."

"Yeah, me too."

When Lynn emerged in the periwinkle dress, Annie nearly fainted.

"You look gorgeous. The blue sparkles highlight your eyes, and your hair looks like it's on fire. Plus, the neckline is sexy, showing off your boobs."

"I didn't realize it had a slit when I saw it on the rack, but I think it works. I just hope I'm not cold while wearing it."

The slit ran up the dress along her leg up to her thigh. It shows off her curves.

"You won't be. There will be hundreds of people at this event. The body heat alone will keep you warm. I love it. You should get it. What about me?"

"I've never seen you so beautiful. That is just the right shade of pink for your strawberry-blonde hair. The red hearts draw the eye to your red lips. If you wear a great lipstick, Sam will not want to leave your side all night," Lynn answered her friend.

The two friends then hunted for the perfect shoes and purses to match the dresses and paid for their items. Because everything was on sale or from clearance, neither went over their budgets. They drove back to their dorm room.

Annie headed off to class. Lynn put on her dress and shoes and admired herself in the mirror. *When Sol sees me, he'll flip. What am I saying? I can't have him. I should have bought the nun outfit. He would have run screaming from me if I bought that one. I don't want that. God, I am horrible. I can't have him at least until one of us graduates. But still, this event is a setting where we can be together without being together. It doesn't matter. I'm not interested in men after Chris, the Russian rapist.*

Lynn decided to take her mind off the reception and Sol and work on the program that is due for her class. She changed back into her jeans, turtleneck and sweater. She was still cold. Interestingly, when she wore the dress and thought about Sol, she wasn't cold. She had an inner warmth. Now that her mind was focused on her classwork, she shivered. She needed him to wrap his strong arms around her. *Oh well*, she sighed.

Sol took the El and trolley home to Upper Darby. He went into his parents house, which was built in the 1920s, but looked modern because of the new paint job and landscaping.

"Mom?"

His mother emerged from the kitchen. She wore pants and an Irish sweater. Sol could tell she just came back from the salon with a fresh brown dye coat on her hair. He kissed her cheek.

"Hi, Sol. What are you doing here?"

"I need to borrow Dad's tux for an event at Penn tomorrow."

"Oh. It's in the attic."

"Got it."

"I'm making spaghetti for dinner. Why don't you stay?"

"Sure, Mom. You know I love your spaghetti.

He climbed the stairs to the attic. As he passed his old room, he noticed his father's gun collection. His father had bought a new case for it. Something tugged at his brain, but it was just out of reach. Something about the collection seemed different, but he shrugged. Sol found his father's tuxedo and brought it down the stairs. He ducked into his brother's room and tried on the garment.

"Wow, Bro. You look like Dad 20 years ago."

Sol jumped and turned toward his brother.

"Jake. Didn't hear you come in the room."

"Sorry. Seriously, you look great."

"Thanks. Penn has a big reception at the library tomorrow. All faculty are expected. I didn't have time to rent one."

The tux was slate gray with an ivory shirt. The buttons were brown like maple furniture and lightened his eyes somewhat. Soon to be 21 years old, Jacob Adams had light brown hair like his mother's and golden brown eyes with green flecks. He parted his hair on the side. He wore a mustache to make his baby face look older.

"How's school?" Sol asked.

"I hate it. My professors dump on me unfairly."

"I doubt that."

"To be honest, I want to drop out. I'm afraid Mom will be against it."

"Probably. But she also won't like paying for something you aren't giving your whole effort."

"I need to talk with her."

"Why don't you change majors?"

"I really don't like school. I like fixing things. I've been going to a technical institute at night to learn how to service HVACs. I think I want to do that."

"Mom will be glad to hear that. She won't use the 'You're-throwing-away-your-future speech' on you if you tell her you have an idea for a career," Sol said.

Jake laughed. "Good point. So are you going with someone?"

"No. I'm not dating."

"I meant to the Penn thing. Are you taking anyone there?"

"No. I don't have time for a social life."

"Bro, you can cut the act. We both know that you don't want to get burned again."

"Jake, you know I don't like to talk about Katrina."

"That's because she's a psycho."

"She just thought there was more to our relationship than there was."

"Sol, stop defending her. She expected you to marry her after three nights of sex. She wouldn't leave you alone even after you told her it was over."

"All right. All right. I don't want to talk about this."

Sol changed from the tux and went downstairs. Jake followed. Both followed the aroma into the kitchen for dinner.

CHAPTER 11
THE RECEPTION

Lynn entered the library. She climbed the stairs to the reception room. She asked the bartender for a soda and grabbed a mini quiche off the tray. She scanned the room. Cookie was flirting with one of her computer classmates. Lynn smiled. *Someone ought to tell Cookie her classmate was gay*, she thought. Lynn couldn't find Sol, not that she was looking for him. Someone bumped into her, and she had to leave. Across the room, Annie and Sam were mingling with Sol. When Sol saw her, his eyes grew wide. He dropped his drink. Lynn couldn't believe how handsome he was in his tuxedo. He was the most handsome man at the reception. She walked toward him.

"You look absolutely gorgeous," Sol said. "I hardly recognized you."

"Thank you. You clean up nice in your tux yourself."

"Ready for the boring speeches?" Sol asked.

"You'll keep me awake like at the re-enactors meeting?" Lynn replied.

Sol laughed. "Of course. I wouldn't want you to fall asleep."

"Then, I'm ready," she said.

When a group of students accidentally bumped Sol, he fell into Lynn. Her leg brushed his and immediately both were on fire. His chest rubbed her breasts, which got her excited. His pants became tight against his skin. He backed away as quickly as possible.

"Sorry."

"I'm not," Lynn said.

Lynn stared into his nearly black eyes and saw a light flash there for a brief moment. She could sense his inner struggle. She felt the same struggle. She rubbed his cheek in an innocent way, but the touch ignited the fire between them again. On impulse, he grabbed her mouth and covered hers with his. Lynn was surprised that she didn't break away, especially with so many people around the room and knowing that she should. Instead, she kissed back. She opened her lips and allowed his tongue to meet hers and probe.

Her entire body tingled with anticipation and excitement. She never felt these feelings before this kiss. She could feel Sol matched her excitement and anticipation. His lips softly held hers and went deeper when she wanted. He put his hands on her waist. One trailed her dress to her soft neck. He caressed her skin as they kissed. Lynn didn't want the feelings to stop. She was flying. She was warm. Annie whispered into Lynn's ear.

"You should stop. The speeches are about to begin, and people might see you and Sol together."

Lynn pushed herself away from Sol, who cursed. "Thanks, Annie."

"I have to go be with Professor Dickenson," Sol said. Lynn nodded. She couldn't speak. Annie grinned a knowing grin. Sam watched the people. Lynn couldn't concentrate on the presentation of the award. Her mind was on the kiss that never should have happened.

"Welcome faculty, students, alumni, family and friends," said University of Pennsylvania's president. "Tonight, we honor a woman who has dedicated her life to the service of the school and its students. We are lucky to have such a wonderful person be here at Penn. I am honored to present this award to Catharine

Stockton, director of library services."

"Thank you, Mr. President. I am glad to be here."

Before she could speak further, an explosion rocked the library. She was thrown from the podium. People ran to the door or were injured in the blast. Sol ran to protect Cookie.

"Sol, what are you doing?" Lynn yelled, but she wasn't heard.

"Cookie, are you OK?"

She didn't answer. Sol covered her with a desk to keep her from getting trampled. The smoke stung everyone's eyes. Lynn looked at Sol one last time before finding an exit.

CHAPTER 12
PANIC

The flames quickly engulfed the room. The firefighters battled the blaze while others rescued the injured guests. Smoke choked his breath, but Sol knew he had to stay with Cookie. He hoped Lynn would understand, but why he cared what she thought he didn't know. He didn't see her in the chaos. He prayed for her safety.

"Sir, you need to leave. Follow this fireman."

"I know," Sol said with tears in his eyes from the smoke. "I just wanted to make sure you found her. Her name is Cookie Stockton. She's badly hurt, but she's alive."

"We will take care of her. Now, go."

Sol nodded. He crawled toward the door following the firefighters. When he got outside the library, he saw the police were having a hard time keeping control. Students were running everywhere screaming. He still couldn't find Lynn. He was worried about her. He headed toward the paramedics location where the firefighters pointed and insisted he go.

The paramedics gave him oxygen and checked his injuries. They were minor, but he was told to go to the hospital. The adrenaline that carried him through the events of the night was leaving his body. He was exhausted and collapsed on the bed in the ambulance.

Lynn arrived at the hospital with the first wave of people who exited the library. She was treated and released. She didn't want to go to her dorm because she would be alone. Annie's injuries were serious enough to keep her in the hospital. She decided to pack a bag and head for home.

"Dad, I'm coming home. I just need to get my car and some clothes."

"Honey, I saw the news. Are you all right?" her dad asked worried.

"I'm OK. I went to the hospital, but I've been released. Annie is still there. It's crazy here. I don't want to be here," Lynn sobbed into the phone.

"See you when you get here. Drive carefully. We love you."

"Love you too."

Lynn jumped into her car and drove toward home in King of Prussia. She avoided the area near the library and took the main roads leading home. Because it was after midnight, the roads were empty. She was home in less than an hour, a trip that normally takes more than 60 minutes. The door opened before she turned the knob. Her father ran to her and hugged her. He held her tight. Tears streamed down her face and his. Her strength evaporated when she was hugged by her father.

"Oh Dad. It's awful." She shook all over her body.

"You're safe now," her dad said. He guided her into the house.

CHAPTER 13
THE INVESTIGATION BEGINS

Special Agent Buck Robertson had his arms wrapped around his young and sexy wife, Angelique, when his cell phone rang. He answered, talked for a few minutes and ended the call.

"Is it about the bombing?" Angel asked.

"Yes. I have to head up the investigation. Such a tragedy. All those people killed."

"I know. We will pray for their souls and healing for those still alive."

"I love you."

"You better get going." She kissed him. "I will pray for you too. Stay safe."

Buck got dressed and headed to the hospital. He wore a gray jacket over his cream-colored sweater. He had a pen and notebook in his hand. He pushed past the curtain to stand beside Sol's bed. Sol looked at him quizzically, waiting for him to speak. Sol sat on the edge of the bed in the emergency room.

"Hello. I'm FBI Special Agent Buck Robertson. How are you?"

"I'm shaken, but not stirred," he answered, trying to lighten the mood.

Smiling, Buck asked, "What's your name?"

"Solomon Adams. Do you know where Lynn Binary is? Did she make it out OK? What about Cookie Stockton? Is she OK? Anyone die?"

"Whoa. Calm down. Right now, I don't know much. Most of the victims are still unavailable to speak. You were the first to be in a state to be interviewed. I do know that Ms. Stockton is in surgery and a Professor Dickenson is dead along with several others, such as the university president and vice president."

"Professor Dickenson died?" Sol said unbelievingly. "I worked for him. I was his teaching assistant. He was to retire in June."

"Mr. Adams, are you OK? Do you need anything? You look pale."

"Please pour me some water."

Buck poured water into a cup by the bed and handed it to him. After a few minutes, Sol looked more together despite his bruises."

"What do you remember?"

"Why is the FBI involved with a local bombing?"

"The Philadelphia police asked for our assistance. Due to budget cuts, the police force doesn't have the resources to tackle something of this magnitude. Also, someone called the tip line threatening a terrorist attack. Now, what do you remember?"

"Well, I remember hearing a hum right before the explosion. I also smelled a weird odor, like dead fish or something. I saw a musket out its case."

"A musket?"

"Apparently, a musket was donated to the university. I'm pretty sure I saw it in a case when I was there before the event."

Buck puzzled over this information while Sol drank more

water.

"How many people attended the reception?"

"I believe around 150. It was open to faculty, students and friends of the library."

"I see. Are you faculty, student or friend?"

"I'm a history graduate student and teaching assistant to Professor Dickenson as I mentioned. I teach Revolutionary War or taught."

"Who do you think was the target?"

"Isn't that your job to determine?"

"Of course, but we like to get ideas from victims."

Sol doubted the special agent but answered anyway.

"All the university big-wigs were there – the president, vice president, PR and other officials. It makes sense to me that they would be the ultimate victims."

"That's our theory too, especially because they are all dead."

"Dead? Wow."

"We have 10 people dead and numerous injured, but we still don't know everyone who was there, and we still are digging through the rubble."

"Can't you get a list of invites?"

"Unfortunately, the people with that information are dead. Our computer people are short-staffed at the moment and busy with an embezzlement case."

"I know someone who might be able to help, but I don't even know if she survived tonight."

Sol frowned. He wished he knew what happened to Lynn.

"How close were you to Cookie Stockton?"

"Not close. I just met her a few weeks ago. I wanted to help her. That's all. Why?"

"Her information lists a Charlie Jenkins as next of kin, but we can't locate him in any database."

"Sorry. I don't know him. I doubt the person is a student."

A nurse entered the area, took his vitals and handed Sol his clothes. She removed the monitoring equipment. She handed him a clipboard with forms to sign.

"The doctor has released you. When you go home, you are to rest for the remainder of today. You can eat or drink regularly. If you have fever, vomiting, dizziness or other symptoms, you must come back here as soon as possible. Do you have a ride?"

"I can give you a ride," Buck suggested.

"I can call my parents or brother. Don't you have to interview others?"

"Yes, but I was going to come back in the morning when more would be able to answer my questions. Besides, I need to get back to the 1776 Inn."

"The 1776 Inn? I was just there for a meeting."

"My wife owns it. She often schedules groups and

meetings to come. Where shall I take you?"

"Graduate housing on Market Street."

"Thank you for your help. Get dressed so we can go. I'll wait for you in the lobby."

Sol climbed into the government vehicle wondering about Cookie Stockton and Lynn. He couldn't stop thinking about the brilliant computer student who looked amazing in her gown this evening. *If she died, I will never forgive myself for not trying to save her. And, Cookie? Why can't the FBI find her relative.* The more he thought about the events of the night, the more his head hurt. He definitely needed sleep. He was so worried about Lynn, though, he probably wouldn't be able to sleep.

"Here you are," Buck announced.

"Thanks Special Agent Robertson."

Sol entered his apartment and plopped on his bed without removing any of his clothes. He was asleep instantly despite his earlier prediction.

CHAPTER 14
COOKIE'S NIECE

Peter carried his baby daughter to her mother. He placed her at Charlie's feet and passed a newspaper over to Charlie and kissed his beautiful wife.

"Why are you giving me a newspaper? I know everything you write."

"This is the phanatic newspaper. Read it."

University Library Bombed at Reception

Last night, a bomb exploded during a reception to honor Catherine Stockton, a long-time employee of University of Pennsylvania. At least 10 people are dead and another 57 are injured. Many more are unaccounted for or believed missing. Philadelphia Police and FBI officials are investigating. They continue to dig through rubble looking for victims. No names of the deceased or injured have been released.

"My aunt? She was bombed?"

Peter sat next to Charlie and hugged her tight. He rubbed her back.

"It doesn't say whether your aunt is injured or dead. What do you want to do?"

"I don't know. What if she is dead?"

"Charlie, everything will be OK. I thought you don't like your aunt."

"We have been getting closer recently since my kidnapping, but anyway, I don't wish *this* on her. She and I might not be best friends, Peter, but I don't want her dead. She did raise me after all – such as it was."

"Honey, I'll go to the scene as a reporter. Maybe, I can find out if she's alive."

"We'll go together. I know how to act phanatic more than you. Your mom or Jill can watch Rosemary."

CHAPTER 15
LYNN'S REACTION

Lynn woke in her childhood bedroom. Her parents have changed the curtains and bedding, but she still felt secure, comfortable and safe. She didn't want to go back to school. She wanted to stay here with her parents and forget the trauma that occurred at Penn.

However, she couldn't shake the image of Sol from her mind. He was covered in soot, coughing and hovering over Cookie Stockton. He had ignored her presence completely when the trouble started. The fact that he went racing to her said a lot to Lynn. *I hope you exploded in that bomb! What am I saying? No I don't.* Despite her anger, she thought about him, craved him and wanted him to wash away her fears. She couldn't have him. He was a teacher. She was a student. He liked Cookie Stockton. Breaking into her thoughts, she heard a knock.

"Come in."

"How are you?" her father asked.

"I'm fine. I'll be down shortly."

"Sweetheart, you had a traumatic event happen to you. Healing doesn't happen overnight. You may stay in your room. You may stay away from school as long as you need to do so," he said as if reading her mind.

"I'll only be a few days. Just until some normalcy returns to the campus," she confirmed.

"Sweetheart, your school had a bombing. I'm not sure that kind of thing goes away too quickly. Besides, there's the investigation to consider. You won't be having classes any time soon. Also, I heard on the news that the campus is shut down until further notice. So, you might as well be here where your mother and I know you are safe."

"I know. Eventually, I have to go back unless I want to quit and give up my dreams."

"I have no doubt you'll find a way to be queen of the computer and rule the world."

Lynn laughed as her father left her room. *Daddy always had a knack for making me feel better and smile.* She dressed in jeans, turtleneck and a sweater. She went down for breakfast and cooked a bagel with cream cheese. The morning sun streamed into the kitchen, which made people think it was warmer than it was. The outside temperature stayed in the 20s, but the sunshine was welcomed. Lynn stared out the window wondering about the bombing. *Who would want to bomb the university? However, lately, crazy people were shooting or bombing everywhere.* She shivered. She didn't want to think about the bombing.

She started thinking about the gorgeous teaching assistant in a tux but then frowned. She didn't want to think about him either. He went to Cookie Stockton as soon as it happened even after he said he wasn't interested in her. And, why should it matter to her? They are adults. They could do as they pleased. She didn't want a man after Chris.

Lynn grabbed her computer and opened it. She wanted to know about the bombing, which was all over the Internet. She saw the death count was up to 12. The number injured has jumped also. She shook her head and cried. So many deaths. She wondered if Sol was OK, but she didn't dwell on it. *I don't care about him. He was interested in Cookie. He wanted to save her.*

Although unsuccessful, Lynn tried to find out who had died. No one had released any names. She told herself that she just wanted to make sure her friends were alive. *Liar.* She hit Annie's number.

"Hey Annie. How are you?"

"I hurt all over, but I'm lucky. I'm alive."

"How's Sam?"

"He has a broken collar bone. Right now, he's laid up in his apartment. So how are you? And, where are you?"

"I'm home. I'm not hurt, just a few scrapes and bruises. Do you know anything?"

Annie sighed. "Just what's on the news, but I do know the FBI was asked to help. No one knows who the bomb was targeting."

"I wish I could do something. I hate feeling helpless. I need action."

"Better not do anything. You could get into trouble for interfering with an investigation."

"Yeah, I know."

But she wasn't convinced.

CHAPTER 16
SOL'S EPIPHANY

Sol jumped up from his sleep. He remembered why the musket bothered him. It was his father's. His subconcious showed him that he realized it was missing. *How did the bomber get his father's musket?* He knew it wouldn't take long before the FBI finds out the truth. Sol figured he would have to tell Special Agent Robertson, but he didn't want his father implicated.

His phone rang.

"Hi Jake."

"My God, Sol. Are you all right?"

"Yeah. Just a little smoke inhalation and a bump on my head."

"The news says the bomb looked like a musket."

"It was a musket. Dad's musket."

"Christ! Are you serious?"

"Pretty sure, but the bomb is in fragments and in custody of the FBI."

"I remembered getting smacked with it when I started playing with it as a kid," Jake recalled. "But to have it used as a bomb, that is even beyond what Dad would have done."

"Dad was protective of that because it was fragile and old. It has been in our family since the Revolution."

"Yeah. I heard the story. Our ancestor fought the British as a soldier. When the fighting ended, he went home and started his family. The musket was handed down from descendant to descendant until Dad. You were going to get it when Dad died. But that might not be a good idea now."

"No. It's in pieces and evidence. At least, the police could tell the bomb was a musket."

"Do the officers know it was Dad's?"

"Not at the moment," Sol said. "I think I have to tell the FBI, but I don't want to hurt Dad."

"Don't tell the FBI."

"Special Agent Buck Robertson will know eventually. Then, it will look like I withheld information and evidence."

"It might not. You could claim you didn't recognize it," Jake surmised.

"OK. I won't tell. At least not now. I have to go. I'm sure the university officials will want to do some type of public relations to help everyone cope."

Sol quickly showered and put on casual warm clothes. He walked to his department head's office to find out what was happening. When he got there, the department was in disarray.

"Good. Sol, you are just the person I want to see," the dean said.

"Good morning. You wanted to see me?"

"Yes. We don't have time to do a full faculty search for a new professor. You will have to be promoted to associate professor and take over Dickenson's classes. You were his TA anyway."

Sol stared at his department head in shock. He couldn't

believe what he heard.

"What?"

"You are to take over the classes."

"But … But, I haven't even gotten my master's yet. I just started."

"We need you to step up to the plate to make the transition as smooth as possible. Can you do that?"

"I suppose, but what about my classes that I'm taking?"

"We will put you on a fast track, removing some requirements. You still will have to present a thesis and do some classes."

"I see. What about the bombing, investigation and Professor Dickenson's funeral?"

The dean explained that the campus was shut down for now and that the office was cooperating with the investigation. That is why the file boxes were scattered all over the floor. Papers were being sorted; books were consulted; and everything was in chaos. He also told Sol that the professor's body won't be released for a week.

"Oh. At 10, the public relations associate will hold a press conference and prayer service for the victims, showing our grief, strength and support. Every faculty member is to attend."

"OK," Sol said. Now, more than before, Sol wanted to see justice done. He wouldn't be in this situation if the bomber hadn't hurt Professor Dickenson. He folded his hands into a fist and pounded the desk. Then, he delved into the file boxes. All the time, he wondered about Lynn. *I hope you are OK*, he whispered to himself.

CHAPTER 17
A HOSPITAL VISIT

Charlie and Peter walked into the hospital.

"Excuse me. I'm here to see my aunt, Catherine Stockton. Can you tell me where to find her?"

The nurse pounded her keyboard and said, "She is in room ICU 14B. Take the elevator to the ICU floor and go to room 14.

They arrived in the room to see the vivacious Cookie lying lifeless on the bed. Too many machines were attached to her fragile body. She looked every bit her mid-life age. Her face was battered and bruised. Bandages covered her wrists. Charlie cried.

"This isn't her. Not the aunt I remember."

"Charlie," Peter said. "She will be her old self again. You'll see. She'll be chasing those men again."

Charlie brought out her wand, but Peter stopped her. "You can't."

"I can heal her."

"You have to let the phanatics treat her. Otherwise, they won't know what happened."

"But I … I guess you are right."

"Try talking to her."

Charlie moved to the bed. Being raised by the aunt who didn't care what Charlie did while she pleasured every man in the universe and Charlie not liking how she was raised made her silent. However, she and her aunt had gotten closer since Charlie's kidnapping and now this happened.

"Um. Aunt Cookie? I know we didn't get along much, but I don't want you to die. I don't want to go through that again."

Peter put his arm around her and rubbed her back, drawing little circles in the center. They both remembered Charlie's story of being orphaned at age eight. Her mother, Cookie's sister committed suicide after her father died of a heart attack. The memories always were painful for Charlie. She was calmed immediately. He looked in her eyes, and they both knew it was time to leave. Charlie gave the head nurse her cell phone number, and they left. Charlie prayed for her aunt and prayed the bomber was caught.

CHAPTER 18
LYNN JOINS FBI

A few days later, a knock sounded on the door. She went to answer and didn't recognize the man at the door.

"My mother and father are out. If you need them, you'll have to come back."

"Are you Floralynda Binary?" asked Buck.

"Yes." Lynn looked puzzled and slightly nervous.

"I am Special Agent Buck Robertson with the FBI. I need to talk to you about the bombing. Your roommate Annie told me you were there that night and that you were here."

He showed Lynn his badge.

"Please come in the house." She showed him to the kitchen. "Would you like some coffee or water?"

"Coffee. Thank you."

He sat down and motioned for her to sit. She sat in the chair opposite him after getting her computer. She thought she might need it.

"How are you?" Buck started. "You have been through a traumatic experience. This will be hard, but I need you to remember."

"I'm OK. I understand. I knew I would be questioned eventually."

"What happened that night?"

"Well, I arrived around 6:30 p.m. The bar opened at 6 p.m. I stood in line to get a soda. I noticed a waiter had just set out the cheese and fruit tray in the room with the rare exhibits. That's where the speeches were going to be. I got to the bar and asked for my soda. I walked around the room to see the silent auction items, but I really was looking for my friends."

"Did you find them?"

"Not right away. I found S.. someone by the food table across the room. Annie and her boyfriend, Sam, were with him talking. I started toward them."

"What happened next?"

"My friend and I started talking about what people were wearing. Everyone was talking and having a good time. Then, I heard a noise, like a loud hum. We also heard feedback before the vice president began talking. He spoke for five minutes. He introduced President Taylor. He spoke for 30 minutes before Cookie Stockton was introduced. She said a few words before the explosion hit. I was standing near the back by the door. I saw people flying backward and running in panic. Mr. Adams, a history teaching assistant raced toward the podium to protect Cookie. I left and went to the hospital before I drove here. I did stop at my dorm for 15 minutes."

"The bomb exploded when Ms. Stockton was on the podium?"

"Yes. Does that matter?" Mr. Robertson had a peculiar look. It's as if he is contemplating something.

"I don't know, but the other witnesses I interviewed never mentioned that. Do you know who was there who might want to kill the president and vice president of the university?"

"I imagine they have enemies, but I don't know. I know

about 150 guests were there, and any student was allowed to attend as long as he or she RSVPed to the Facebook group."

"The library computers are a mess and our computer tech staff people are still working several embezzlement cases and trying to get an invite list."

Lynn typed on her computer and pulled up the Facebook group page. Although it was closed and locked by an administrator, she typed some more and pulled up a list. She showed it to Mr. Robertson.

"Amazing. Are you able to print that list?"

"Sure. I just need to send to my parents' printer. These are two lists, the invites and the responses. You can focus on the ones who said yes. I realize that some of the yeses might not have attended, but it gives you a starting point. I have always been a whiz at computers. I am studying programming. I want to create video training games using wearable technology," Lynn announced. She retrieved the lists for Special Agent Robertson.

"How about a paid hacking job?"

"Hacking job?" Lynn asked.

Mr. Robertson smiled. "Officially, you will join the investigating team as a freelance computer expert because our workers are doing other cases, but, in reality, you'll be hacking. Are you interested?"

"How much?"

"How about $100 an hour throughout the investigation. Of course, you'll have to file a W9 form."

"Mr. Robertson, it sounds like you just hired yourself a hacker." She stuck out her hand. Buck shook it.

"Fantastic. Oh and you may call me Buck. Before I forget, I hired a history professor for this investigation too."

Lynn shivered. "Who?" she asked although she knew the answer.

"Mr. Adams. Thank you for your help. Come to the 1776 Inn tomorrow morning for details. I sometimes telework. My wife owns the inn and is booked for the week due to the President's Day holiday that just past. She needs my help. Bye now."

Lynn felt like she had been stabbed in the stomach. She had to work with the gorgeous TA who had a thing for Cookie Stockton and saved her over Lynn whom he had just kissed. He didn't even care if she had lived through the bombing. And, a kiss she can't forget. She will have to be strong and hide her feelings. She can't pass up $100 an hour job.

CHAPTER 19
DUTY CALLS

Sol walked into the 1776 Inn to meet FBI agent Robertson. He was met in the foyer by a beautiful young woman with shiny black hair and hazel eyes. She smiled.

"Welcome to the 1776 Inn. How may I help you?"

"I'm here to see Special Agent Buck Robertson."

"My husband is in the cellar getting me some supplies. He is meeting in the dining room. I am Angelique Robertson, owner of the 1776 Inn."

She motioned for Sol to follow. The last time he were here, he sat in a conference room. He walked into the pleasant dining room that was painted a mint green and decorated with red, white and blue flowers in a Lincoln's hat on a dining table that was a replica of one in the Revolution era. It was polished and shone. The table had no scratches or nicks on it. A lace runner finished off the decoration of the table. But, the décor wasn't what made Sol stop short. With her back to him, Lynn sat at the table with her laptop opened in front of her. His heart jumped at seeing her. Sol was relieved that she was alive and safe, but he also felt a burst of lust even though she wore a turtleneck and a sweater over jeans. He wondered why she never called him to tell him she made it out the library OK. Angelique's next words brought him back to the situation at hand.

"Buck requested Ms. Binary to attend this meeting too. Would you like me to introduce you?"

"No thanks," Sol replied. "We know each other."

"Then, I'll leave you to go fetch Buck. Have a good day."

Sol walked to the other side of the table to greet Lynn.

"I'm glad you made it out OK. No one was able to tell me," Sol informed her.

"Mr. Adams, Mr. Robertson said you were coming," Lynn cooed coldly.

"Mr. Adams? I thought we were past that."

"That was before you rushed to save Cookie Stockton."

Sol smiled. *Lynn was jealous*. This was good news to him because he liked her. He wanted her around him every way possible. He can't stop thinking about her and that kiss. His lust just shot up another notch. *Stop it*, he told himself. He had feared she died before he got to know her. He is glad he was wrong. The joy that filled his heart when he saw her just shows how much he wants to get to know her.

"We have to work together now, so I'll have to be more businesslike," she said, but Sol didn't hear her.

"I went to Ms. Stockton because I have been raised to help. She would have been trampled to death. She means nothing to me."

"Fine. Whatever." Clearly, she didn't believe him or trust him.

"Lynn, don't be like this."

"I'm just trying to be civil so we can work together."

Sol came to her chair, yanked her from the seat and held her close to him. He kissed her with all the anger, fear and frustration he felt for her. The passion exploded from him to her. She kissed him back with just as much anger and frustration. Soon their passion heated other parts of their bodies. Sol inched toward her, forcing her breasts to rub his chest. He fondled her left breast through the sweater. She moaned. His other hand held her face and caressed her cheek sliding down her neck. Lynn wrapped her hands around his neck and moved to his cold and thick hair. She played with the strands and deepened the kiss. Sol felt his arousal growing and pressed closer to her jeans.

"You are so beautiful," he said to her hair.

"Sol …" was all she could reply.

Her hands slid from his hair to his chest. His first two buttons were undone. She slipped her hand inside the shirt. The cold flesh quickly heated under her touch, and he kissed her more. She leaned closer. Sol fondled her breast some more. She moaned again. He loved that sound. Lynn broke the kiss and pushed back. He looked at her wondering.

"You are still a teacher. I am still a student. And, we have this meeting right now."

Sol felt as if someone had hit him with a snowball when she uttered her words. The reminder of their statuses was as good as if he walked in a blizzard or went back outside the inn. Their situation was worse than previously because now he was an associate professor instead of a teaching assistant. Lynn didn't know of his promotion. He realized that he has to keep his hands and lips to himself and off her. He can't have her. She's a student. He could choose so many other women, but none of them was Lynn. He couldn't understand what made her so special to him, make him want her so much, but she did. He prayed that God gave him the strength he needed to avoid trouble with Lynn.

He went back to his side of the table and sat. He could endure her presence as a business associate. Just when he was sure his arousal was gone, Buck entered the room.

"Thank you both for coming here instead of the FBI office

downtown. I often work here, especially when Angel needs my help. What I need from you is this. Ms Binary, I need you to go through everyone on the invitation list even those who declined and check out their backgrounds. Write down everything even if you think it's insignificant. I want to find any connection the bomb might have to any of the university personnel from President Taylor to Ms. Stockton. Can you do that?"

"Absolutely. I can create a computer program that runs in the background and pop up a link. That way, I can do other work and my schooling."

"Perfect. Mr. Adams, I need you to discuss muskets. Where do people buy them?"

"Only from museums or collectors. A search on Ebay will come up with a few, but a serious buyer will go to auctions or gun shows."
"Are there a limited number of places?"

"Yes. The historical gun world is small, about a dozen main players. Of course, the bomber could have stolen the gun or purchased it illegally."

"If the musket were stolen, how would we know?"

Sol needed to tread lightly. He didn't want to give away that his father's gun was used. Lynn typed on her computer and showed Buck the screen. It was for a historical gun registry site.

"You can plug in a serial number, and if it was reported stolen, this site will tell you," she said.

Sol kept his frustration from showing on his face. "All the serial numbers are in that database even the ones that aren't stolen. Do you have the serial number?"

"No. The blast eliminated it. We are using chemicals to try

to retrieve it, but my guys tell me several numbers are missing, which will make it difficult to identify that way."

Sol sighed with relief. "Well then, talking to major players is the only way to go. I can do that. I'm often consulted for authenticity. My grandfather collected. My father is a collector. I'm starting to collect."

"Good. Do some research so we can get a better handle on how it was managed. Also, I need you to research any historical significance the ideas of a musket bomb might have to the library or the date. You are both free to go. Thank you again for your help."

Both got off their chairs and asked the housekeeper for their coats. They walked into the cold air thinking about the passion that occurred and how it would warm their insides about now, but they can't have it.

CHAPTER 20
PLANS AND ALERTS

Katrina reveled in the aftermath. Everyone at the university was scared. All the people who had a hand in the firing are dead. She didn't know about whether Cookie Stockton was alive. An added bonus, which she didn't know before she planned this, was that her ex was at the reception and got injured too. He didn't die, though.

The dirtbag should be dead! How dare he sleep with that slut Cookie Stockton when he was supposed to be with me forever.

Katrina remembered his strong body and sleek arms wrapped around her voluptuous form. She remembered his soft hands as they caressed her legs and arms. She remembered the dates. He stared into her eyes over dinner, rubbed her back at the museum and touched her lips after eating a hot dog. It was magical. Katrina remembered how he dumped her like trash for Dumpster bin.

He claimed he felt nothing. He lied. Feelings were there. I wouldn't let it be over. That's why I followed him and when I saw him having sex with that woman, I nearly screamed. Damn him! He must pay!

Katrina turned on her computer searching for gun dealers. She needed another musket.

Lynn decided to go back to the campus. She needed to get caught up on her work even though most classes were canceled for a week. The library was still closed. Doing computer programs would take her mind off what happened with Sol.

Why can't I control myself around him? I see him and

immediately my desire is so strong.

She walked into her dorm and sat at her desk. Before she turned on her computer, Annie entered. Lynn jumped and gave her a hug.

"How are you, Annie?"

"My scars are healing, but the memories won't leave. I have nightmares of people screaming and running for the door. I'm so glad I can rely on Sam. He has been my rock during this."

"I know. Being back here has made me think constantly of that night. I needed to get back to work, though. Keeping busy gets my mind off that night." *And other things.*

"Yeah. Classes resume tomorrow. The university is having a memorial service this afternoon. Are you going?"

"I think it is necessary to pray for the victims and those still in the hospital. I also want to pray for Special Agent Robertson who is handling the investigation, so I'm going."

"I'll join you. Hey, did you hear?"

"What?"

"Mr. Adams has been promoted to associate professor as Professor Dickerson's replacement. The poor man died in the bombing."

Lynn stared unbelieving at Annie.

"What? When did this happen?"

"Two days after the bombing."

Lynn thought. *That means he was an associate professor*

when I saw him at the FBI meeting, when he fondled my breasts. God, I'm a fool. To hell with him for lying to me.

She shook her head. Time to put the professor behind her. She could work with him, but she wasn't having sex with him.

"You'll never believe what happened, Annie."

"What?"

"The FBI hired me to research stuff for the bombing investigation. Mr. Robertson said his computer experts were working another high-profile case, and he needed a computer expert."

"That's great! If you can't find the information, no one will."

"Thanks. I'm working with Mr. Adams."

"Really? Now, you'll be able to get to know him better."

"Strictly business, Annie. You just said he is an associate professor now. The rules are tougher between professors and students than between TAs and students."

"He might be an A. P., but he's only 23. And, he likes you."

"Annie, stop playing matchmaker."

Lynn moved to her computer and switched on the laptop. She stared at her screen. At her puzzled look, Annie came over to the laptop. It was beeping an alert.

"What's that?" Annie asked.

"I created two programs. The first sends me an alert when

someone searches for gun dealers. The second looks for links among university staff, employees and those invited to the party. This alert means someone is looking for gun dealers."

"Click on the alert. Let's see what you found."

Lynn tapped a button, typed a password and the notification popped on the screen. It listed an IP address and search results for gun dealers who sold 1776 muskets. The user name of the searcher was Madam K. Nothing else was on the screen.

"Do you know who Madam K is?"

"I have to hunt down the IP address and search the user name. It will take me a few days to figure it out, but the problem is Madam K is trying to buy a 1776 musket. It might be a coincidence, but I don't think so. I think Madam K is looking to create another bomb."

Annie crossed herself. "Oh my God. You better tell the FBI."

"I agree. The problem is I have no information to give Mr. Robertson."

Annie got bleached white as she realized what Lynn was saying. The second bombing could happen at any time by a nameless Madam K, and they were helpless to do anything about it. Lynn sat at the computer and began to hunt down the IP address and said a prayer she found the bomber in time.

CHAPTER 21
TRACKING THE GUN

"Associate Professor Adams. How can I help you?"

"Sol, it's Jerry."

"Hey Jerry. It has been a long time."

"I know. So what's so urgent?"

"You hear about the bombing?"

"Who hasn't?"

"The FBI asked me to contact gun dealers to track the sale of a 1776 musket. You were my first call."

"Interesting that you mentioned that. I got a call today asking if I got any in stock. I don't, but the person was too in a hurry to wait two weeks for me to get one. I told her to try Historical Guns."

Sol flinched. *This was not good.*

"Seriously? Someone called today?"

"You sound surprised. I thought that's why you called."

"It is and I am," Sol sighed, not quite keeping the fear from his voice. "The FBI wanted me to track the original gun sale, which I don't have to do because, between you and me, the gun was my father's. And, if someone called today ..."

"Christ! Someone might be planning another bomb!"

"I know it might be a coincidence, but I don't believe in coincidences, especially so close to the first one."

"I agree, Sol. It looks bad."

"Did you get a name?"

"Sorry, Sol. We didn't get that far. She hung up after I told her Historical Guns, but it was definitely a woman. You could call over there."

"I'll have to do that."

"Sol, God be with you. Hope you catch the bomber and find the gun."

Sol ended the call and sat at his desk thinking. Before calling Historical Guns, Sol punched Lynn's number.

"Hello."

"Lynn, don't hang up. I know you are still angry."

"Professor Adams. What can I do for you?"

Sol grimaced. *She knows. She is more angry now.*

"OK. I deserved that. I should have told you. I didn't think when I saw you at the meeting. All I knew was how beautiful you were and wanted to kiss you."

"Did you want something? I am quite busy."

"It's about the case. I think another bomb is planned. Did you find anything?"

Sol heard a pause and a sigh. He waited.

"I think so too."

Sol stopped before asking, "How?"

"Someone named Madam K searched for gun dealers selling 1776 muskets. I'm still tracking the IP address. I didn't tell the FBI because I don't have enough information."

Sol absorbed this information with his own.

"Sol, are you there?"

"Yeah. I'm still here. Do you know a target or timeframe?"

"No. That's what's scaring me."

"Me too. I know it will be less than two weeks given what I was told from a friend of mine. I have another call to make. Let's meet for dinner to discuss our findings." *This is not a date. It's two business associates having dinner. Just dinner. Not a assignation in my bedroom.*

"Sol, I don't know. We could get caught. I'll be kicked out of school."

"Lynn, it will be OK. I really like you. Just dinner."

Despite what he said, he knew it wouldn't be OK. He was lying to himself.

"Meet you at Olive Garden at 8?"

"Sounds great."

Then, he called Historical Guns.

CHAPTER 22
COOKIE WAKES

Cookie blinked awake. Her entire body hurt and not the good hurt, the one she enjoys. She looked around the room and realized she was in a hospital. She saw Charlie sitting in a chair asleep.

"Charlie," she whispered. Her mouth was dry. "Charlie," she said again.

Charlie blinked and looked at her aunt.

"Aunt Cookie." She jumped to her bedside.

"Get me some water."

Charlie poured some water and put a straw in the cup. She moved the cup to her aunt's mouth to let her drink.

"That's better. What day is it?"

"Feb. 19. You have been unconscious for five days."

"Have you been here the whole time?"

"No. I was coming here when I had a break at work or home. Peter has been hunting down what information he can and taking care of Rosemary."

"What do you know?"

"Not much. The FBI believe the target was the president of the university. There are no leads, but a student and a professor have been hired to help with the investigation," Charlie summed up the story.

"A professor and a student?"

Charlie nodded.

"Must be Solomon Adams and Lynn Binary. You need to heal me so I can leave. I don't feel safe here."

"Aunt Cookie, you know I shouldn't do that, but I'll take away your pain."

Charlie waved her wand over her aunt and removed her lingering pain.

"You should heal naturally in a few days. It will appear less odd that way."

"Thank you. I still don't feel safe here. What if I am the target?"

"Why do you think someone is after you?"

"I have been with a lot of men. One of them or one of their wives could want revenge."
Charlie thought a minute. "I suppose it's possible, but I have seen you breaking up with men. They always left with a smile. I don't see the motive. You will need to talk with Special Agent Buck Robertson anyway. You should tell him your concerns."

"OK. Is there anything else you can do?"

"I can place a personal shield charm on you, but that will not protect against weapons or bombs. It will protect you if someone is using magic or nonlethal attacks against you."

"Do it."

Charlie said an incantation and a warm glowing circle engulfed Cookie who felt better.

"Aunt Cookie, I'm sorry this happened and that I missed your special night. Had I been there …"

"You might have been killed."

"Or I might have saved you and stopped the bomb."

"Sol Adams saved me."

"Is he your latest?"

"Just a friend. Once was all either of us wanted."

Charlie grinned for the first time in days.

"I'll leave you to rest, but I'll tell the FBI to visit you."

"Charlie, I do love you even if I don't show it."

Charlie remembered how her aunt would leave her alone most of the time so that she could spend time with her latest guy. She also remembered how upset her aunt was when Charlie was kidnapped. She shook her head. Her aunt loved her in the only way she knew how to love.

"I care for you too."

When Charlie left, Cookie stared at the ceiling and thought. Several hours later, the door opened and an FBI agent entered.

"Ms. Stockton, I'm glad to see you awake. My name is Buck."

She liked his strong muscles and lean physique.

"Can you tell me what you remember?"

"Not much. It happened so fast. I walked on the stage, adjusted the microphone and barely got out my greeting before the explosion hit. Sol grabbed me and protected me until we could escape. I woke up here."

"Did you see anyone suspicious?"

"No, Sugar. Anyone at home?"

"I am happily married Ms. Stockton. I know your reputation."

"Pity. You are one beautiful piece of meat."

"Back to the case. Do you know who might want to harm anyone there?"

"I have been thinking that the bomb might have been directed at me because of my reputation.

Buck was surprised she thought that. He had been considering the possibility.

"How so?"

"Revenge. But I don't know who it could be."

"Do you know a Madam K?"

"No, but I know a Katrina. She is a book store employee who has been upset that I fired her brother. He didn't work hard enough. He made mistakes. He was caught stealing. She has complained I didn't give him a chance."

"That's interesting. Is she dangerous?"

"I don't know her that well. Why?"

"A Madam K has been interested in muskets. We think another bomb is being made. We have no more information than that."

"Another bomb? Good Lord! You think Katrina and Madam K might be the same person?"

"We don't know at this point, but the similarities are interesting and there is the revenge motive."

"Well, in that case, I will pray you catch the bomber whoever it is in time."

"Thank you, Ms. Stockton. Get some rest." He left leaving Cookie to begin to worry that he might be right.

CHAPTER 23
REVENGE IS SWEET

Katrina acquired the musket and materials she needed for her second bomb. She began the painstaking task of putting together her masterpiece.

Where shall I place this one? I can't have it in the open or it will be found. I need a special place. I need to make them pay!

She went back to work visualizing the maximum damage. The office would be the most logical choice, she decided. She smiled, happy that her plan was coming together. Everything will be OK. As she worked she thought about that day at Rutgers where her life fell apart. She thought she was special until she heard him talking to her friends.

"Katrina has a nice body, but something is off about her."

"Are you breaking up?"

"We have been on three dates. That's hardly a relationship."

"She told my sister that you were the one."

"I don't understand why she thinks that. I haven't event been faithful. I went out with Carla too. I have to end this now."

Katrina couldn't believe what she heard. He was unfaithful and said, "Something was off?"

She pounded her fist. She will get her revenge. *No one will have him, least of all Cookie Stockton!* She continued. Time to put her plan in action.

CHAPTER 24
THE TARGET

Lynn walked into Sol's office. Every time she saw him, she had to catch her breath. He was more handsome the more she saw him, but he was even more off limits now that he was named a professor. Today, he wore black jeans, a white shirt and a red sweater. His outfit complemented her cream turtleneck, black pants and a sweatshirt with Penn's logo on it. His heat radiated the office and all through her body. She wasn't cold. She wanted Sol's warm body. *Off limits, remember?*

"Hey Lynn. What brings you here?" Sol asked.

"I came across some chatter about people turning muskets into bombs. Apparently, Madam K has quite the following."

"That's scary. Has Special Agent Robertson or you figured out her identity?"

"No. That's what's so frustrating."

She tried to hide her fear in her eyes, but she noticed that Sol saw it anyway. He stood, grabbed her and held her. He rubbed her back. When she looked into his eyes again, she saw that his desire reflected her own. His lips touched hers lightly. The sparks ignited the passion that always simmered between them. Their bodies melted together as fever raged through their bodies. Lynn broke the kiss just as Sol was reaching under her turtleneck.

"Sol, this can't happen."

"I don't care about the rules. I want you so damn much."

"It is more than the university's rules. We have to find a killer. And, I don't want to disappoint my parents. They want to see me wait for my husband. They are extremely old-fashioned and religious. I want to be at least through school before I have sex."

"Very well," he sighed. "Speaking of the killer, Madam K visited one of my associates looking for 1776 muskets. She is searching for a specific one."

"Damn."

"My reaction exactly."

"I wish I could find the target for the next bomb."

Sol stood still, a weird expression on his face. He smacked his head.

"What is it?" Lynn questioned with fear taking over her eyes again.

"The target. You just reminded me that the original targets couldn't have been the president and big wigs of the university."

"Why?"

"Because, if they were the targets, Madam K wouldn't need to make a second bomb. That means that the target must be someone who has survived."

"Oh my God! I hadn't thought of that."

"The only person who makes sense is Cookie Stockton."

Sol piled books and papers into his briefcase. He pushed Lynn out the door.

"Where are you going?"

"I have to warn Cookie, and you have to tell Special Agent Robertson."

Lynn felt her frustration return. Of course, he wanted to race to Cookie Stockton. She was glad she stopped Sol's advances before she made a mistake. She was glad he was a professor. She was glad she felt nothing for the handsome history professor even though she was lying to herself. She might have fallen in love with him, and he wanted Cookie. Lynn walked to her dorm while Sol jumped into his car and sped away. Lynn pulled out her cell phone to call the FBI.

CHAPTER 25
SLEEPLESS NIGHT AT THE INN

Buck caressed the side and hip of his sleeping naked wife, Angelique. He loved looking and touching her. He remembered how he almost lost her. Now, he feels lucky to be with her, but his job still scares him that something like the bombing might happen and risk her life. He can't live without her by his side.

He continued to caress her and moved his hand along her back and down her buttocks. That woke her.

"Buck, as much as I am enjoying this, it's three in the morning. I need to sleep. I have to be ready with breakfast by six for the guests."

"I know, but you have only five people and Dad. It won't be a problem if you are later than normal."

"It is winter. The five came here for Valentine's Day and leave in two more days. Still, I want them to enjoy themselves."

"They will. You are a great B&B owner."

"Buck, what is bothering you?"

"This case. I got a call from my computer expert that she and Associate Professor Adams figured out the target is Cookie Stockton. I'm worried that we won't figure out who Madam K is in time and more people will die."

"You will. I have faith in you."

"I don't want to be the reason people die."

"Everyone dies sometime, but you are good at what you do. God gave you talent to solve the puzzle so you can prevent people from dying before He wants them to come home."

"I just feel lost, out of my element. How can I solve this puzzle?"

Angelique smiled her brilliant smile that always took Buck's breath away and gave him peace. Then, she licked his shoulder, and he responded.

"Thought you were tired."

"You need this. It is the only way I will be able to get you back to sleep."

Buck nodded. He pushed her on her back and entered her. Soon, both were satisfied and sleeping. He dreamed of himself catching the killer.

CHAPTER 26
SIX DEGREES OF CONNECTIONS

"Lynn? Are you here?" Annie asked as she entered the programming building.

"I'm in the back."

Annie walked toward Lynn's voice. When she found her friend, she smiled.

"I have been looking everywhere for you. I didn't think you had gone home again."

"No. Just wanted to be in a place where no one would disturb me."

"You mean Professor Adams. He has called the dorm four times. I thought you were working the bombing case together."

"He has called and texted my cell too. Yes, we are working the case together. I still don't want to talk with him."

"Why are you avoiding him?"

"I can't get in a relationship with him. He is a professor now."

"A relationship? I thought you were just working together."

"Well, we might have let our hormones get the better of us a few times."

"You mean that you ..."

"No, not that. Just kissing and fondling. Every time, I think about the case, I remember how good his hands felt. I get distracted. Plus, he is older and done school. I'm not."

"He's in graduate school. Hardly done school. And, he is only four years older than you. I think you two have something in common."

"Yes, it's called Cookie Stockton."

Annie frowned.

"What do you mean? Did you find out about him having sex with her?"

"What?!"

"Apparently, not. So, what are you talking about?"

"The night of the bombing. He kissed me passionately. Then, he raced to save her. In his office last week, he raced to go to her after fondling me. Now, you tell me he had sex with her? I am sooooo over him! He is nothing but a womanizer."

Annie studied her friend and saw the pain in her eyes, pain caused by strong feelings.

"You aren't over him. You like him a lot. Maybe, you should give him a chance. Listen to what he has to say."

"No. He could rot in hell for all I care. Let him save Cookie. I'm done."

She stomped past her friend just as her laptop pinged an alert. Lynn froze. She slowly turned and looked at the screen.

"What is it?"

"It's my program that tells me connections of people at the university. Christ. Listen."

Katrina Romanov works at the university bookstore. Although she does not work with Catherine Stockton in the library, they often work closely together regarding curriculum committee assignments. She also dated Solomon Adams and expected to marry him when he ended the relationship after three dates. Christoph Romanov worked for Catherine Stockton for six weeks before being fired for low-quality work and theft. Christoph and Katrina are brother and sister.

"Christoph, isn't he …?" Annie started.

"Yes. My ex-boyfriend who tried to rape and choke me. God, Annie. Do you know what all this means?"

"That everyone is interconnected?"

"Yeah, and Katrina must be Madam K. She wants revenge against Cookie for firing her brother, against Sol for dumping her and against me for dumping Christoph."

CHAPTER 27
ECSTASY IN THE DORM

"Shouldn't you tell someone?" Annie asked.

"I will tell Special Agent Robertson, but right now, I have to get to class. And, we still don't know when."

Lynn turned off her laptop and left the computer programming building for the sociology building. As she sat in class, she forgot about the program's results. She kept imagining Cookie having sex with Sol. Every time she thought about it, she got angry.

How dare he? He told me I was special. But, what am I saying? I don't want to get into a relationship with him. I need to focus on my studies. Was that how he saw me? As just a student that a history teacher can conquer? I was right to stop talking to him. OK, we do have to talk about the case, but I can use Special Agent Robertson as the intermediary. I don't need to talk with Sol.

Lynn couldn't concentrate on class. The professor's words just washed over her head. Someone tapped her shoulder. She looked at the person, questioningly.

"Class is over, Lynn. You have to leave the room," the student said before leaving.

Lynn scanned the room and saw everyone had gathered their books and were walking out the door. She was so distracted, she didn't know it ended. She grabbed her laptop and backpack. She was the only one left. Before she could get out the door, Sol stood in front of her.

"What are you doing here?"

"I looked up your class schedule."

"What? Why? That's an invasion of my privacy."

"Lynn, you won't answer my calls or texts."

"That's because I don't want to talk with you. Run along to Cookie." Lynn turned toward the door.

Sol grabbed her arm to turn Lynn to face him. "Lynn, she is a friend. I saved her because I don't believe in leaving people who are hurting if I can help. I had to warn her about the bomb. Turns out she already suspected she was the target. I don't have feelings for her more than a fellow human being."

"Is that why you jumped her bones?"

Sol grimaced. Lynn smacked him with her backpack. She wrenched her arm free and turned again for the door. Sol blocked her path.

"Lynn, look at me. I'm telling you the truth. She means nothing. The sex was just an opportunity, nothing more."

"You are nothing but a womanizer, ready to take anyone who is available."
"No, I won't."

At that, fire filled her gaze. Anger was still there in her eyes, but it mixed with the real desire she felt for this man who is willing to forego sex to respect her beliefs. She pulled his head to hers and kissed him, then bit his lip.

"Ow."

"Just leave me alone." Lynn stormed toward her dorm. Sol caught up with her.

"Look, I had meaningless sex with her because I was frustrated over my desire for you. I want you, but I understand your feelings and you are a student. I know I can't have you. I respect your beliefs. I respect that you want to wait, and your parents believe in the sanctity of marriage. I don't want you to break God's commandments or go against your beliefs. I am a lowly sinner. I know I can't have you, so I settled for Cookie."

Lynn smiled. The way Sol listed her principles and his respect for them made her see that Sol was different from other men. Most of the time, they call her a name and march away or try to rape her to get what they want. Lynn told Sol about Christoph. Sol turned angry. She was ready to find Christoph and pummel him into the ground for what he did or almost did to Lynn. She touched his arm. Sol relaxed.

"I respect all the reasons why you don't want to have sex, but I have to have your smile, your voice and your laughter. I have strong feelings for you. We don't have to have sex, but there are things we can do."

Lynn realized she was back at her dorm. She opened the door and brought him inside the room. Lynn knew that Annie wasn't going to be back for several hours as she had back-to-back classes and then planned to meet Sam. So, she kissed him. She grabbed his jacket and pulled him closer. Sol responded instantly. Soon the anger turned into passion. Lynn twirled her fingers through his hair. Sol found her breast and caressed it like he never caressed another breast. She moaned. He groaned.

"You are wearing too many clothes," Sol blurted.

"It's winter, and I'm cold."

"Are you cold right now? Let me warm you, Lynn."

"Mmmm. I like how you warm me."

Sol placed his jacket on the chair. He took off Lynn's coat and threw it on the floor. The hat and gloves followed. Sol wrapped his arms around her.

"I have imagined what your sexy body looks like under the jeans and turtlenecks. Let's get rid of these layers," Sol said.

He lifted her shirt and yanked it from her pants. Lynn pulled at his belt. Sol lifted his shirt over Lynn's head. Lynn shivered partly from the winter air, but mostly from the desire for Sol firing her blood. She reached for his zipper and moved it down the seam. Sol shimmied out his pants and snapped the hook on her bra. He guided her to the bed and laid beside her. When her breasts were free, he took a breast in his mouth and suckled. Lynn moaned.

"You are so beautiful, Lynn. Before we go any further, how much of this do you want?"

"I want some of it. I ache for you. Your legs are strong, and you are warm."

She pulled at his shirt. Sol quickly removed it and threw it into the pile of clothes on the floor. He unzipped her jeans and slid them down her slender and muscled legs. He removed them slowly, making her feel every sensation as he got lower. She moaned again.

"We'll stop when you say" and took her other breast in his mouth.

She inhaled his scent of clean male and a hint of musk. She panted as he worked on her breasts. He massaged the other. She moaned again. Sol enjoyed her sounds. Lynn circled her fingers on his scalp, then in the hair on his chest. She played with his nipples. He threw back his head in delight. He watched her body react to his touch and her touch on him. He moved his hand down her torso, memorizing every inch of her body. She shivered again from the pleasure. Pulling his mouth from her breast, he said, "Let's get under the blankets."

Although his heat was taking over her body, she complied with his request and felt like she fell into a furnace. Sol kissed her again on her mouth. Lynn invited his tongue to enter her mouth and played with it until his lips moved to her neck and ear lobes. He licked his way down her body to her belly. She writhed beneath him, making the bed shake and the blankets twist. His hand followed his lips. He slipped his hand into her panties and massaged the chestnut curls over her sensitive skin. He entered her opening with two fingers. Lynn jumped from the shock but was caught by the blankets and pleasure. He coaxed her back to where his hand worked its magic on her sensitive nub. As he rubbed, the pressure mounted toward a climax. Lynn saw stars and blue skies when the climax hit. Sol watched her and felt his penis harden more than it had been.

"God, Lynn."

Lynn grabbed his penis through his boxers and stroked his shaft. She kept moving up and down the long length. Sol's breathing quickened. He leaned back to give her more access. His face was full of rapture. He moaned and kissed her.

"Lynn," he repeated.

Lynn brought him to his knees and let the rapture envelop him. It took him in full force. Sol exploded in his underwear. Both laid in each other's arms for a long time.

"I better go," Sol said.

"I know, but you can wait a while."

"All right," he choked.

They cuddled and talked. They talked about her dreams, his family, her beliefs, his faith, their problems and the forces keeping them apart. They didn't talk about the case and their fears.

Sol kissed her cheek. "I have to go now." He gathered his clothes and put on his jacket. As he walked out her room, Lynn whispered, "Sol I love you." She wasn't sure he heard her.

As he left, a woman watched him from the shadows. Her anger over seeing him coming from a girl's dorm incensed her. *Soon, my cheating fellow. Soon.*

CHAPTER 28
FRUSTRATION

"We don't have enough for a warrant," Buck said.

"But Mr. Adams and Ms. Stockton are in danger," Lynn pleaded, "Not to mention me."

Lynn sat in the FBI office with Special Agent Buck Robertson, showing him what her program found – that Katrina Romanov is connected to Sol, Cookie and herself. She tried to convince Buck that Katrina was Madam K and to take action to stop the next bombing.

"Ms. Binary, I agree with you. My gut already told me Ms. Stockton was in danger. I also agree that you and Professor Adams also might be in danger. I know you are right about Katrina being Madam K. The problem is we don't have anything to connect her to the bombing. All we know for a fact is that she purchased a 1776 musket after the first bomb, which has not shown up in our serial number tracking, yet. Thus, we can't get a warrant. Can you connect her to the first bombing?"

"Other than her obvious dislike of us? No."

"Exactly. We don't know where the first musket originated, who had it and who put it in the library. We need to be extra careful on this case or a good defense attorney will get a judge to throw out the evidence. Then, she will walk right out the door to possibly bomb again."

Lynn sighed. "I understand, Mr. Robertson. I'm just so frustrated and am feeling helpless. What should we do?"

Buck stood and walked to the window. He stared out the window with his back to Lynn. She admired his muscles and straight back. His sandy brown hair blew from the air in the heater. He turned.

"When she was in the hospital, we could give her protection, but now that she has been released, she has to accept it. She has refused our 24-hour protection. We are adding extra men to the university. They are undercover at the places Ms. Stockton frequents. Based on your data, we'll put some at your dorm and at the history building. We could give you protection if you choose."

"I would like that and for Annie too. My roommate."

"I'll order it." He sighed. "We don't know when she will strike or where. It makes our job harder."

Lynn considered that for a moment.

"That's assuming she will want to take out Cookie without trying to take out us. What if she wants to get rid of all of us at the same time?"

Buck stared at Lynn.

"That makes sense. Do you know when the three of you will be together at the same time? The bomb would have to be placed somewhere that is public enough to get all of you. The library is out because of the damage already done. No one is going there for a while."

"The only place that would get all three of us at the same time is the Student Center. That is where everyone goes to eat. Even if we can figure out the where, we don't know when. It has to be a time when all of us will be in the same place," Lynn reminded him.

"Not necessarily. She could force you to be together, which would make the when more urgent."

"You mean like an invitation?"

"Yeah, like that."

"I got a message from Sol to meet him in his office at 3 p.m. He said Cookie will be there to discuss the case and what she knows about Katrina."

Immediately, Lynn jumped from her seat at the same time Buck raced to his desk and grabbed his gun.

"We have to get to the university!" they shouted together.

CHAPTER 30
BOMB IN OFFICE

Sol threw his briefcase on his desk. He had a trying day of classes. His students protested outside his classroom. They didn't think they should be forced to take classes so soon after the bombing. They didn't feel safe. They didn't want to be bothered to take notes. The students punched and kicked him as he past them to enter the room. None of his students arrived. They were too afraid.

He went to the Student Center for coffee only to have someone bump into him and he spilled the coffee all over him. A colleague berated him on his stance of a particular revolutionary battle.

He was tired because he wasn't sleeping due to the bombing case and Lynn. He wanted her so much. Sol heard her whisper that she loved him, but he thought that it is just what every 19-year-old girl says. *It doesn't mean anything.* Yet, he can't stop thinking about her. His feelings for her are strong. *Are they love?* He didn't think so. Because she whispered it, Sol didn't believe she was even sure about her feelings either. He just wanted to get through this day and go home. The bright spot of the day was the text Lynn sent that told him to wait for her in his office. She was coming to him and bringing Cookie to discuss new developments in the case.

Then, he saw it. A long, thin package sat on his desk. He looked at the door. He thought he should just go and have the package scanned. He was about to leave when Cookie walked into the room.

"I got this note from you that you wanted to see me about the case, Sugar."

"I thought you were coming with Lynn."

"Why would I do that?"

"Because that is what Lynn told me."

Sol looked at Cookie alarmed. He realized the text didn't come from Lynn but was made to look like it came from Lynn. And, Cookie was brought to his office under false pretenses. He stared at Cookie, looked at the package and back at Cookie. He never said a word.

"Why are you looking at me like that?"

"Cookie, we have …"

Slam!

The door banged shut. Sol ran for the door. It was blocked. Cookie now realized what was happening.

"We need to get out of here," Sol breathed.

"How? You have a window with no way down."

"We must find a way."

"What can we do?" Cookie asked with panic creeping up her spine. "Is that …"

"I believe so. I believe that if we unwrap that package, it will be a 1776 musket made into a bomb. Check my closet. I think I have my rock-climbing gear in there."

"Rock-climbing? We are on the fifth floor of a high-rise building. How are we supposed to climb?"

"Do you want to stay in this room to be blown to bits? Do you have a better idea?"

"Not really." Cookie looked in the closet and found the rope but no handholds. "We have rope, but the other equipment is missing."

"Damn that woman!"

"What woman?"

"Madam K, the person behind the bombings. Let's tie the rope to the filing cabinet. It should be sturdy enough."

Cookie remembered her knot-tying class she took to be able to use in the bedroom and went to work. Sol looked for anything that might help them descend the building. He pulled out his phone and saw his battery was too low to call Buck. His desk phone was missing and his computer was smashed.

"Do you have a phone?"

"No. Your note told me not to bring one. You didn't want to be disturbed. Now, I think that was odd."

"It wasn't my note. We have no way of calling the police or fire department."

"So, this rope is all we have?"

"Yep. I don't even know how long we have before the bomb explodes."

"We have another problem."

"What?"

"The windows' glass are designed not to break and don't open."

"Crap. I forgot."

"What should we do?"

A knock sounded at the door.

"Sol, it's Lynn. Your door is locked with a computerized mechanism and is blocked by a table."

"Lynn, if you are here because you think I asked you to come, leave now! I didn't ask you here, Madam K did," Sol ordered.

"I know that Katrina Romanov lured all of us here. I'm with Special Agent Robertson. I will have to hack it to get the door released. It will take awhile."

"Lynn, you need to leave!"

"Did she say Katrina Romanov?" Cookie asked.

"Shsh. I need quiet."

"Lynn, the bomb is on my desk. You need to leave and be safe," Sol said with fear gripping his insides.

"Mr. Adams, we know about the bomb. I have called the police and bomb squad. We are trying to get through the door so the bomb squad can dismantle it," Buck said calmly.

Sol looked at Cookie. He was more confident, but he still wasn't sure they would have enough time. Cookie was frightened. She held the rope in her hand so tight her knuckles were white. He rummaged through his bag for anything to help. Then, he registered the name, Katrina Romanov. He smacked his head.

CHAPTER 31
42 MINUTES TO WORK

Lynn sat by the door with her laptop beside her. She accessed her program that detects frequency. The software located the frequency of the lock box. She activated the command to search.

"Now, it will look for the combination and passwords to open the lock box."

"How long will it take?"

"I don't know. Sometimes, it finds the code quickly. Other times, it takes hours."

"We don't have hours," Buck cautioned.

Lynn swiped the hair from her eyes, clearly nervous. "I know. I will work as quickly as possible. We need a miracle. We should pray for all of us that this works."

"Mr. Robertson, we have not detected any signals that might suggest a remote control," an FBI agent reported.

"That must mean the bomb is on a timer. Mr. Adams, is the bomb on a timer?"

"I never unwrapped the package. I was going to leave when Ms. Stockton entered and then, the door slammed shut."

Buck considered. "She must be near. Go search. Mr. Adams, unwrap the package, please."

He heard rustling. Lynn gripped her computer, sweating greatly.

"There is a timer on the musket."

"When will it explode?"

"We have 42 minutes."

"Not a lot of time, but better than five minutes. Mr. Adams, we are working to get you free," Buck said.

Lynn kept her head down. She had to focus on her task. If she thought about the danger, … *No she must believe Sol will live.* She said a prayer to her guardian angel and kept up a stream of Hail Marys. She continued working to release the lock. Her palms soaked with sweat, and her hair lost its shine. For the first time this winter, she wasn't cold. Her concentration broke when an agent ran up to Mr. Robertson.

"Sir, we found clothing in a janitor's closet, but she's gone."

"You checked the whole perimeter?"

"Yes, sir."

"OK. Take the clothes to the lab."

"Yes, sir."

"Ms. Binary, it's all on you to get this opened."

"I know. I'm working as fast as I can."

She wanted to collapse. Her fingers hurt so bad. She was thirsty from the perspiration and fear. She kept working, knowing she had to save Sol.

"Hold this like that," she heard Sol tell Cookie. "Mmm. That's good."

"You think this will work?"

"Of course, it will work."

Anger replaced her fear. *How dare Sol do that while she worked super hard to free his sorry ass?*

"No, not that way. Like this. Yes, that's it. That feels right." *Damn him!* Lynn thought.

"Shouldn't we wait?" Cookie asked.

"We have 30 minutes left. Do you really want to wait?"

"No, let's do it."

Lynn shook with anger, fear and intense concentration. She had to get the door opened. She had to stop them. Then, her miracle happened. A woman with blonde hair the same as Cookie's appeared in the corridor. She was careful not to be seen by any of the agents. Lynn saw her briefly wave something at the door. She disappeared a moment later.

CHAPTER 32
CUTTING GLASS

Sol couldn't believe he had that quartz and geode in his bag. He found them in August when he took the rock-climbing trip. He sharpened the rocks on the letter opener on his desk. Now, they could cut the glass on the window. He told Cookie the truth. It would work, but he didn't know how fast. She was so pale. He had to give her hope.

Now, both stood by the window working the lines of the glass, trying to cut it, so they could climb out the window. While he has faith in Lynn's computer skills, he wasn't sure she could do it in time. This was his Plan B, alternate.

"Mr. Adams, Katrina disappeared."

"Katrina? What about her?" Cookie asked.

"You know Katrina?"

"She worked at the university in the campus bookstore. She wanted me to hire her brother, which I did, but I had to fire him."

"She's the one behind this."

"I thought it was a spurned lover. Wait, how do YOU know her?"

Sol sighed. "I had the misfortune to take her on three dates before dumping her."

"That's why we are both stuck in here. She wants revenge against both of us."

"It appears so. Let's get moving. We have 23 minutes

before her revenge is realized."

Just as Sol heard a break in the glass, he heard a loud beep. Then, the door burst open. Lynn ran into the room ready to strike someone, but she skidded to a halt when she saw Sol at the window completely dressed. Cookie was behind him holding a rock and rope in each hand. She realized that what she thought she heard was something else. Relief flooded her, and she ran to hug him, not caring if people saw.

Buck followed with three men and women who were wearing protective gear. They went to the bomb. Buck's man looked worried.

"Sir, these wires are interwoven. If we cut the wire that disables the bomb, it will explode. If we don't, it will explode in 10 minutes.

"Crap."

"We could throw it out the window," Sol suggested. "I just got the glass cut."

"If we do that, we could injure people on the street or residents in the neighborhood. How far is the chemistry building?"
"It's on the other side of the campus. We wouldn't make it."

Lynn and Cookie both paled as they listened to the conversation. They knew what it meant.

"Sir, we have a suggestion. We could try to remove the clock mechanism. If we stop the clock, we should stop the explosion."

Buck considered for 30 seconds. "Do it. Mr. Adams, Ms. Stockton and Ms. Binary, you have to leave. Follow me. Team, take cover."

They dropped the rocks, grabbed their purses, computer and wallet and followed Buck out the door and down the hall. Lynn and Buck said a prayer for the bomb squad. After 10 minutes, when they didn't hear anything, they all sighed with relief. A man ran up to them with an evidence bag with the bomb parts.

"Get that to the lab. We need fingerprints and other identifying evidence to arrest her. We also need a match to the bomb fragments of the last bombing," Buck said.

"Mr. Robertson, there is something you should know. The first musket was my father's. I couldn't understand how my father's gun was used and I didn't want him arrested, so I didn't tell you. Now that I know Katrina is behind this, I can tell you. She was at my father's house for dinner on one of my three dates. She must have stolen it then," Sol summarized. "I'm sorry I withheld evidence."

Lynn stared at him and glanced at Buck who showed no emotions.

CHAPTER 33
THE PLAN

Katrina ran. She had to disappear. The FBI is after her. She didn't know how their workers connected her to the bombs, but they did. Now, she needed to get as far from the university and as far from Philadelphia as she could.

She knew public transportation would be watched. She had a plan. She would head to the river and hire a boat, but not a cruise ship, which wouldn't be there in February anyway. She would take a fishing charter and be lost at sea for weeks. Then, she could head South. She prefers the warmth.

Eventually, she would have to finish what she started. For now, she must leave. She punched a button on her untraceable cell phone. A car arrived to take her to the river.

CHAPTER 34
THE CAPTURE

After what happened at her inn last year, Angelique was more aware of her surroundings and people looking suspicious. So when she stood on her balcony for fresh air on the sunny and moderate winter day and saw the woman at the river looking like she didn't belong, she called Buck.

"I don't know what she's doing, but it doesn't look good," she told her husband.

"Does she have straggly brown hair that tangles in the back, a round face with a scar and a short stature?"

"Exactly like that."

"Angel, talk with her. Keep her there. I'm on my way. She's the bomber," Buck told his wife. "Be careful not to let her know you know."

"You want me to talk with a bomber?" Angelique was incredulous.

"You won't be in danger if you don't reveal that you know. She won't know who you are or what you know, but if you don't keep her on the dock, we might lose her again. Have faith that God will protect you until my team will get there in five minutes. Love you."

"OK. I will talk to a bomber." Angel laughed because that is all she could do in a situation like this.

Angelique grabbed her winter coat and walked down the steps toward Penn's Landing. She headed for the woman looking for something.

"May I help you? You look lost."

The woman was startled at Angelique's words. She showed fear briefly in her face and stance, but she quickly recovered.

"Oh. I'm looking for a fishing charter. I want to try commercial fishing for a book I'm writing," she said.

"All the charters leave before five in the morning. They fish all day and arrive around 7 p.m. in the evening. You are too late for today. However, I own the 1776 Inn and would be happy to have you there while you wait for tomorrow's fishing charters. You can tell me about your book."

"I don't have any money for your inn."

Angelique was puzzled.

"Then, how were you going to pay for the charter?"

The woman was once again fearful and startled. She cursed her flawed speech.

"Well, I have enough for the charter, but I don't have any extra."

Angelique changed the subject.

"Today, is nice for a winter day. Don't you think?"

"Yes, nice. That's why I thought about the fishing. I thought the water would be warmer and calmer."

"You said it was part of book you were writing."

"Yes. The book is about a number of professions. I picked a nice day for the calm waters to get research for the fishing chapter. So, do you think the water is calm enough to try fishing?"

"I suppose. I don't go on boats much. I am just starting to do some pleasurable trips."

"Why is that?" the woman inquired without realizing that she was extending the conversation.

"My father died while rescuing a family, and my mother stood in the rain watching him, caught pneumonia and died too, but it was a long time ago."

"Sorry about your lost. I lost my brother. He disappeared. I hope he's alive, but I really don't know."

"So sad."

Sirens could be heard in the distance. Angelique looked behind the woman as if she was seeing across the river into New Jersey, but she was really watching Buck's car.

"So, have you looked for him?"

"Yes, in the beginning, but he has been gone for two years. He might have gone back to Russia where we lived."

Buck was walking toward them. The sirens were getting louder. With his eyes, he signaled Angelique who understood.

"Are you planning to go to Russia too?"

"I'm not sure. February is frigid in Russia. I would rather go to Florida or Bahamas."

Buck pointed his gun at Katrina's back. "Katrina Romanov, you are under arrest for the attempted bombing of a history office and the attempted murders of Solomon Adams and Catherine Stockton."

He grabbed her hand before she could react and put handcuffs on her. Angelique walked to her inn before Katrina could turn to look at her and connect her to Buck. Police sirens blared from the street, providing the backup needed, but Buck had everything under control. Later, he kissed his wife.

"I am always amazed at how brave and calm you are when facing danger. I love you."

"Don't make me do that again. I nearly died a thousand deaths because my heart was racing, but I love you too."

The couple snuggled under the covers in their suite and made love.

CHAPTER 35
SO CLOSE, YET SO FAR

"I'm glad it's over," Lynn said to Annie.

"Yeah. Now, you can focus on Mr. Adams."

"Annie, Sol is still a teacher."

"I thought you told me it didn't matter. That life was too short."

"I do think so, but Sol and I aren't meant for long-term. He doesn't want a relationship."

"Are you sure? I see how he looks at you. And, didn't you say you got together?"

""We haven't had sex, but yes, we came close. I think he is happy with a fling."

"Are you?"

"No, Annie. I love him, but what can I do? I have to finish school and he is going for his master's."

"Tell him how you feel."

They walked in silence to their classes. The wind whipped through their clothes. *I hate being cold*, Lynn thought. *Sol is warm. I want to snuggle up to his warm body*. She sighed, but it sounded like a chipmunk's chatter due to the cold.

Sol sat at his desk, reading papers. It had been so long since he assigned them, long before the first bombing. He forgot what they were supposed to write in the papers. He got distracted from the work by the case and Lynn. Then, his office was a crime scene for couple more days. He is glad he can finally get back to them. And, he needs the distraction from thinking about the luscious body of his computer expert.

What am I to do about her? I want her all the time. A fling is not going to work. I heard her whisper. I know she loves me. It was probably the situation. If we went for a long-term relationship, what could I offer her? We are both in school.

A knock sounded at the door. His brother entered.

"Hi. What are you doing in town?"

"We heard the FBI caught the bomber. We wanted to know if you are OK."

"Physically? Yes. Mentally? Not so much."

"Yeah, finding out your ex caused so many deaths can be mentally nerving."

"It's not just that."

"What else is wrong?"

"I like a girl, but I don't know what to do about it."

"Who?"

"You don't know her. She's a computer student."

"How old is this 'student'?"

"She's 19, Smartass!"

"OK, she's legal. What's the problem?"

"The problem is she just started college, and I'm going for a masters and have been named an associate professor. The university has a policy against professors dating students."

"Don't let the university find out about it."

"I think eventually someone will know. And, I want more than a fling. I want to get to know her."

"Ah. Someone's in love," Jake teased in a sing-songy way.

"That's not true! I hardly know her. Look what happened when I didn't wait until I knew a woman before I slept with one?"

"Katrina's a pyscho. She never was right for you, but the way you gush about this one, I'd say it's right. And, I doubt you can meet two psychos in a row."

"I know. I survived even though the psycho wanted me dead. Now, I see life is short. You are probably right about Lynn, but I'm going to end it before it goes further."

"Why would you do that? You should see where it goes."

"I don't see how I have a choice unless I transfer to a different school."

After Jake left, Sol went back to his papers, but he still thought about Lynn. He pictured her silky chestnut hair, rosy cheeks and curves hidden under all those layers of clothes. He remembered how she felt beneath him. He thought about what he said and shook his head. Although only four years separated them, it might as well be 40.

CHAPTER 36
HOSTAGE SITUATION

When he got to Annie's paper, he thought about Lynn some more. He decided it was time. He pulled out his phone and punched in the numbers.

"Lynn, meet me for coffee? But not on campus. Let's go to Liberty Place."

"Sure, Sol. I can get there in 30 minutes."

At the coffee shop, Sol smiled when he got a glimpse of Lynn. She was wearing her ski jacket, a hat low on her face, a plaid scarf around her mouth and nose, and woolen mittens. She walked toward Sol in her thick pants and winter boots. Despite the winter clothing, Sol watched her body move in graceful and sexy glides toward his table. At that moment, he knew his brother was right. He loved her. Yes, it was true. He loved her intelligence, her courage, her willingness to help others and her sexy body. He respected her faith, beliefs and principles.

Before she reached the table, though, she was tripped by a worker. Her scarf was snagged on a table corner. Someone stepped on her scarf that trailed the floor from the table. She rolled into a chair and hit her head. She sat rubbing her head.

Just as Sol was breathing a sigh of relief that Lynn was OK, a new danger emerged. One customer got off his chair and blocked her way and wouldn't let her stand. Sol sat frozen to his seat not sure what was happening or what to do.

"Well, if it isn't Floralynda Bitchy."

"Don't call me that."

"Why not? It's your name."

"You know I don't use it. I thought you disappeared. What do you want?"

"What I want? You ruined my life and my sister's life, and you ask what do I want? Bitch."

He yanked her hair so she stood. Sol jumped from his seat, but before he moved toward them, the man pulled out his Glock gun. Sol stepped back.

"Chris, what are you doing?"

"I'm going to kill you and everyone here."

Pandemonium took over the coffee shop. People screamed; dishes crashed to the floor; baristas and customers ran for the door; and Sol was pushed farther from Lynn. Chris shot his gun at the ceiling. The noise deafened all those who were near, including Lynn.

"No one leaves!" Chris shouted.

Everyone moved to the farthest corner, blocking Sol yet again. He was beginning to panic. *I have to get to Lynn.* But, with the crowd blocking his way, he called the police so Chris wouldn't see him do it.

"You entice me with your body, reject me and call the cops? You get my sister thrown in jail and me fired. You have ruined me. Now, I will ruin you."

"Chris, I didn't reject you. You raped me. Your sister got herself thrown in jail." Sol was trying to figure out who the sister was when Chris shot his gun again.

"Shut up!" He grabbed her arm, ripped the jacket sleeve. He yanked her hair again. "You don't talk again unless I say so!"

Lynn trembled. She tried not to show her fear and her head pounded in pain. Sol inched closer to Lynn. He needed a plan. These things were always easier in the movies.

"You ruined my life. You don't deserve to live."

A customer whimpered somewhere near him. Chris shot his gun a third time and hit the customer in the shin. Everyone screamed again. At that distraction, Sol got Lynn's attention. He conveyed his meaning without words. She barely nodded, but he knew she understood. He whispered to a staff worker. He crawled toward his target. Chris leveled the gun at Lynn again. Sirens sounded up the street.

"Just shooting you is not enough. I have to make you suffer as I have suffered."

He took out a pen knife and sliced open her jacket. Then he sliced her turtleneck down to her jeans. He grabbed the fabric with his slimy fingers to push aside her clothes. Just before he got to her bra, he was pushed. Lynn kicked him as he flew backward. Sol tackled Chris. They fought. The gun skittered away. A customer stepped on it to keep it from Chris. The two men rolled and crashed into tables and chairs. Chris swung his arms. Sol punched and avoided the blows, but some hit his face or gut. Sol was so angry he grabbed Chris' head and slammed it against the wall. Chris slid into a puddle on the floor. Sol kept pummeling him.

"You have no right to touch her that way." Punch.

"She's mine." Punch.

"You lost your chance when you attempted to rape her." Punch.

"You will never come near her again." Punch.

A soft hand touched his arm. She turned his face toward hers.

"Sol, stop. He's unconscious, and police officers are coming. You don't want to kill him."

Sol heard the words, but he was filled with adrenaline and couldn't stop. Lynn tried again.

"Sol, it's OK. Look at me. I am fine."

Sol looked at her and around the shop. Everyone stared at him wondering if he were the crazed man instead of the one with the gun. He pointed to the worker and moved away. The worker had a butcher knife in his hand and stood over Chris. The police entered the scene. The worker put the knife on the counter. Lynn ran to Sol's arms. Sol removed Lynn's ripped jacket and draped his over her so her ripped clothes would be covered.

"Lynn, are you OK?"

She nodded. "I'm just frightened. This has been a difficult month."

"It's over now. I think it's truly over."

"What happens now?"

"We get married."

"We get married?"

"The university allows students and teachers who are married."

"I'm a freshman."

"We can work out the details. I almost lost you twice. I

don't want to have it happen again without my telling you how much I love you. I can't live without you."

The coffee shop erupted in cheers. The police officers clapped. Lynn radiated her smile at Sol.

"I love you too. When you were trapped in that office with a bomb and Cookie, I couldn't bear it. Yes. I will marry you!"

Everyone cheered and clapped again. The police officers pulled her aside to question her and Sol.

CHAPTER 37
FAMILY MEET AND GREET

"Why don't you like your name?" Sol asked while holding her and comforting her in her dorm.

"It's too long and difficult to pronounce."

"But, it means beautiful flower. You are a beautiful flower, my flower. The prettiest!"

"Thank you, but computer engineers are not flowers."

"Why can't you be both? The way I see you, each part of you is another petal that makes you who you are. My perfect rose."

Lynn was taken back. She had never thought of herself in those terms before Sol said something. She frowned.

"We can't marry."

"What? Why?"

"Sol, I am a freshman who lives in a dorm. Where would we live? How would we live? How can we afford marriage and school?"

"Lynn, you are just afraid. Let's let love and God show us the way. We will talk with our families. I am sure we will come up with a solution."

She smiled. "Sounds like a plan, I guess."

"Don't worry, Beautiful Flower."

In Lynn's family living room, Lynn, Sol, her mother and father discussed the situation.

"So, let me get this straight," her father began. "You want to get married, get our blessing and find a way to stay in school?"

Sol nodded. Lynn's mother slapped her husband.

"Can't you see they love each other? I think it is so romantic and beautiful."

"Well?" Lynn was anxious.

"You have our permission and blessing," Lynn's mother gushed.

"Now, wait. How can you support our daughter?"

"Pedro's store, of course!" Lynn's mother exclaimed.

"Who is Pedro?" Sol asked.

"My uncle. He runs an antique store that specializes in outfitting restorations of historical homes. That is perfect. Why didn't I think of that?" Lynn bounced as she said it.

"Yes. He needs a history expert to authenticate eras in homes and to do marketing for the store and clients. You will be perfect. He'll even pay for your master's degree tuition," Lynn's mother also said with a bounce.

"I don't need my master's degree paid. The university is paying for it because I was promoted to associate professor. I also have that salary and have a trust fund my grandmother started when I was a boy."

"A trust fund? Why didn't you tell me earlier?"

Sol blushed. "It's enough for college but not much more than that, and it didn't come up."

Lynn's phone rang. She looked at the screen and answered.

"Special Agent Robertson, what can I do for you?"

"Lynn, my superiors were impressed with the work you did on the case. They want to hire in our investigations department. It would be part time until you get your computer programming degree. Are you interested?"

She was shocked, placed the phone on speaker and asked Buck to repeat what he said for everyone to hear. They all clapped.

"I would love that. Thank you."

She ended the call.

"Well, now we have figured out how you will support my daughter and her schooling," her father continued. "Where would you live?"

"As a professor, I am entitled to faculty housing. Currently, I'm on a waiting list. I have a one-bedroom apartment right now. It would be cramped, but OK for now," Sol answered.

"You are a professor?" her father asked.

"Well, not really. I was named an associate professor to finish out the semester for Professor Dickenson's classes where I was a teaching assistant, but to remain after June, I have to have a master's degree and three years as an assistant professor. Therefore, I have kept my TA salary, which is so small, until I can achieve those goals. Yet, the rules for housing don't have those restrictions. Most of the faculty want them."

"Do we have any family members with property in the city?" Lynn pleaded.

"Sorry, *Querida*. We don't," her mother lamented. "Enough sadness. It is time to celebrate!

They ate, drank, danced and celebrated the engagement into the evening. The next day, they visited with Sol's family.

"Whoa, Bro! Last week, you wanted to dump her. Now, you're engaged?" Jake argued.

"You showed me what I had, and the psycho killers showed me what I could lose," Sol answered matter-of-factly.

"Leave him alone. It is beautiful. She is beautiful," his mother said.

"Sure, Mom."

"Thank you," Lynn said.

Sol and Lynn told his family the plan for financial support and going to school. They explained they planned to marry at the end of March in Lynn's church with the reception at the 1776 Inn. Lynn mentioned her family was planning an after-the-honeymoon party in the summer for all her cousins and aunts and uncles because they needed more time to plan that big event. Sol's family will be invited for that bigger event too. For the March wedding, they wanted only immediate families. It had to be as quickly as possible to be allowed by officials at Penn.

"How exciting! Welcome to the family, Lynn!" his mother gushed.

"Where are you going to live?" Jake asked.

"Daniel is looking for a buyer for his condo in Center City," his mother offered. "We could give you the money as a wedding present."

"A condo?" Lynn got excited. "Who is Daniel?"

"How big is it?" Sol asked.

"Three bedrooms, two baths, right on the El line. He is moving to New Jersey with his new wife who has two kids in school in Cherry Hill from a previous marriage. He said even though the condo is in a good part of the city, people don't want to own in the city. He has had a tough time selling it," his mother summarized. "Daniel is Sol's cousin."

"It sounds perfect for us!" Lynn gushed.

"When you let God direct your path, everything works right," Sol preached with love showing toward his bride-to-be and to God.

Later that day, Lynn and Sol visited an antique store to find the perfect ring from the Revolutionary War era to serve as Lynn's engagement ring. Lynn saw a band she liked for a wedding ring. She just couldn't find the perfect one to be her engagement ring. Sol took her back to her dorm. When he visited Pedro's store to meet his new boss, he saw a ring he liked and thought she would too. It showed a kite made of a stone to match the color of her eyes with a lightning bolt of diamonds in the center of the kite. Sol bought it. When Sol showed it to Lynn, she gasped.

He said, "It represents beauty and electricity. You are beautiful and need electricity to be an expert in computers."

"I love it. Without Ben Franklin, I would not be able to do what I do. I love you so much."

They married in March. Their wedding night was the explosive exploration of their bodies that they predicted that night in her dorm. Their love for each other and their happiness meant that Lynn was no longer cold even in the winter. Lynn continued to attend classes. Sol doubled his class load to get his master's degree sooner. He worked for the university and for Pedro. She worked for the FBI. Together, they worked to find solutions to their obstacles and challenges. Sol continued his hobby of re-enactments. Lynn always attended to watch her husband and father enjoy themselves. Every day was a blessing and a gift.

Angelique's inn continued to be successful. Both Buck and Angel were delighted to learn she was pregnant. Buck continued to catch criminals for the FBI. Charlie Jenkins and her aunt Cookie rekindled their relationship. Cookie Stockton considered giving up her flirtatious ways, but her flirting resulted from an incident that she never told her niece. She just thought it might be time to let go of the past and embrace the future.

Thank you for reading *The 1776 Musket*. I hope you enjoyed it. Please write a review on Amazon. Stay tuned for *The 1776 Soldier*, the next in the series. Sol's ancestor meets Buck's ancestor while a modern crime is investigated.

Sincerely,

Louise Harris

www.ingramcontent.com/pod-product-compliance
Lightning Source LLC
Chambersburg PA
CBHW020621120726
47905CB00003B/883